SUPER POTATO

#9 SUPER POTATO'S ALL-NIGHT DINOSAUR FIGHT

ARTUR LAPERLA

Graphic Universe™ • Minneapolis

Story and illustrations by Artur Laperla
Translation by Norwyn MacTíre

First American edition published in 2022 by Graphic Universe™

Graphic Universe™
An imprint of Lerner Publishing Group, Inc.
241 First Avenue North
Minneapolis, MN 55401 USA

For reading levels and more information, look up this title at www.lernerbooks.com.

Main body text set in CCWildWords. Typeface provided by Comicraft.

Library of Congress Cataloging-in-Publication Data

Names: Laperla (Artist), author, illustrator.
Title: Super Potato's all-night dinosaur fight / Artur Laperla.
Other titles: Super Patata (Series). English
Description: First American edition. | Minneapolis : Graphic Universe, 2022. | Series: Super Potato ; book 9 | Audience: Ages 7–11 | Audience: Grades 2–3 | Summary: "When Malicia the Malignant sends dozens of dinosaurs to fight Super Potato, the number of prehistoric pests keeps him awake for days. How do you defeat a T-Rex on 42 hours with no sleep?"— Provided by publisher.
Identifiers: LCCN 2021047113 (print) | LCCN 2021047114 (ebook) | ISBN 9781728424590 (library binding) | ISBN 9781728462950 (paperback) | ISBN 9781728461014 (ebook)
Subjects: CYAC: Graphic novels. | Superheroes—Fiction. | Potatoes—Fiction. | Dinosaurs—Fiction. | Humorous stories. | LCGFT: Superhero comics. | Humorous comics. | Graphic novels.
Classification: LCC PZ7.7.L367 Stn 2022 (print) | LCC PZ7.7.L367 (ebook) | DDC 741.5/973—dc23/eng/20211006

LC record available at https://lccn.loc.gov/2021047113
LC ebook record available at https://lccn.loc.gov/2021047114

Manufactured in the United States of America
1-49328-49444-12/10/2021

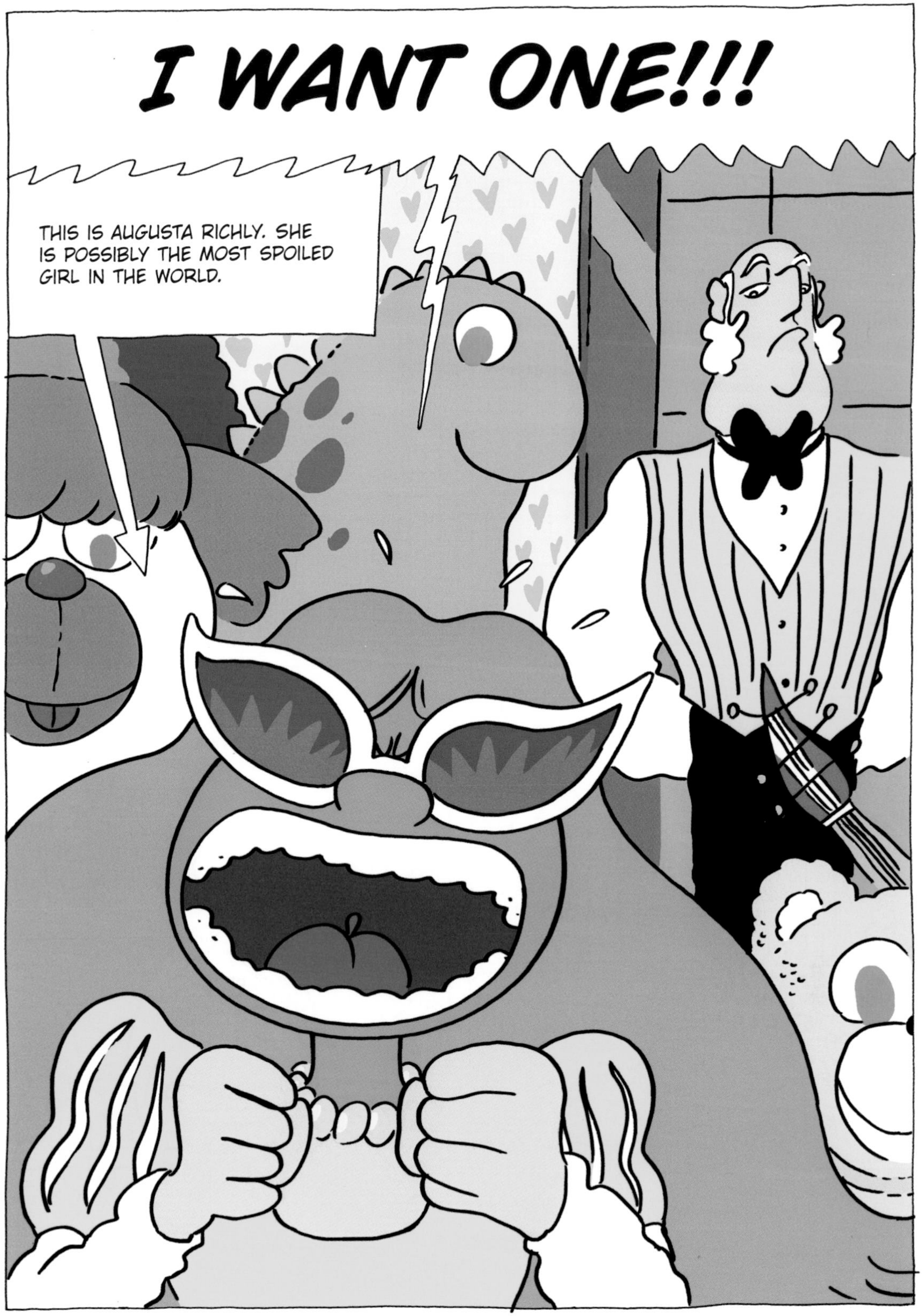
I WANT ONE!!!
THIS IS AUGUSTA RICHLY. SHE IS POSSIBLY THE MOST SPOILED GIRL IN THE WORLD.

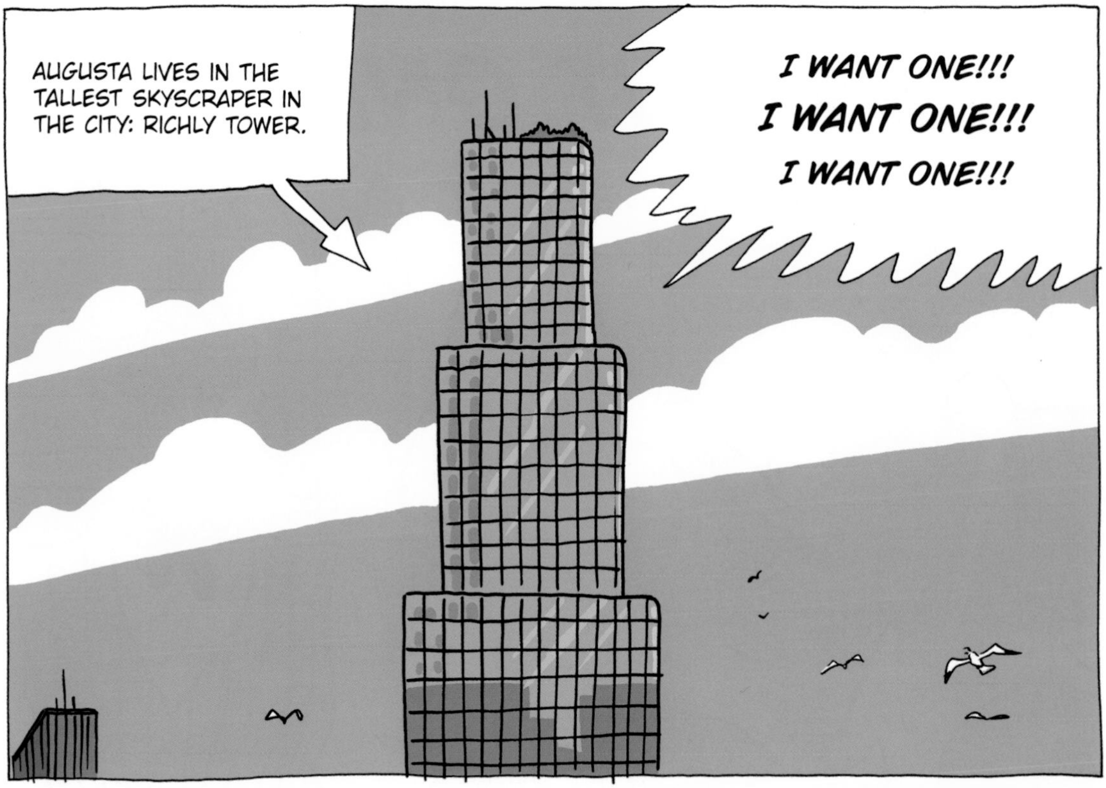
AUGUSTA LIVES IN THE TALLEST SKYSCRAPER IN THE CITY: RICHLY TOWER.
I WANT ONE!!!
I WANT ONE!!!
I WANT ONE!!!

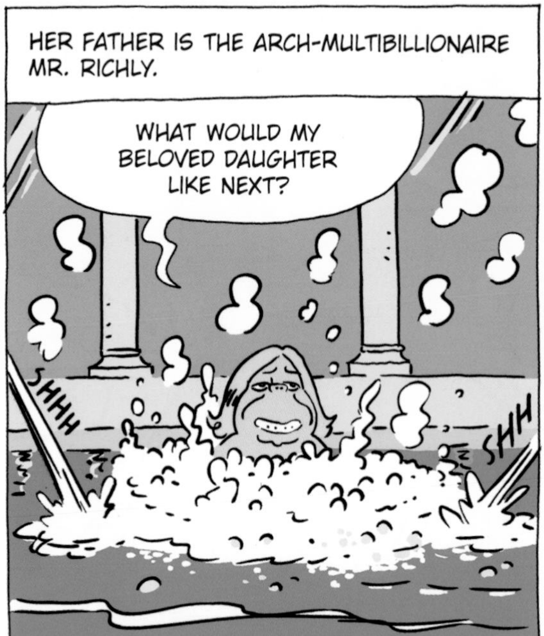
HER FATHER IS THE ARCH-MULTIBILLIONAIRE MR. RICHLY.
WHAT WOULD MY BELOVED DAUGHTER LIKE NEXT?
SHHH
SHH

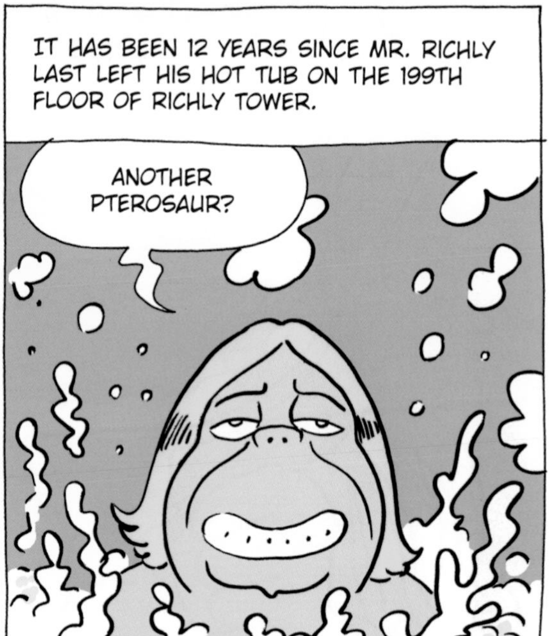
IT HAS BEEN 12 YEARS SINCE MR. RICHLY LAST LEFT HIS HOT TUB ON THE 199TH FLOOR OF RICHLY TOWER.
ANOTHER PTEROSAUR?

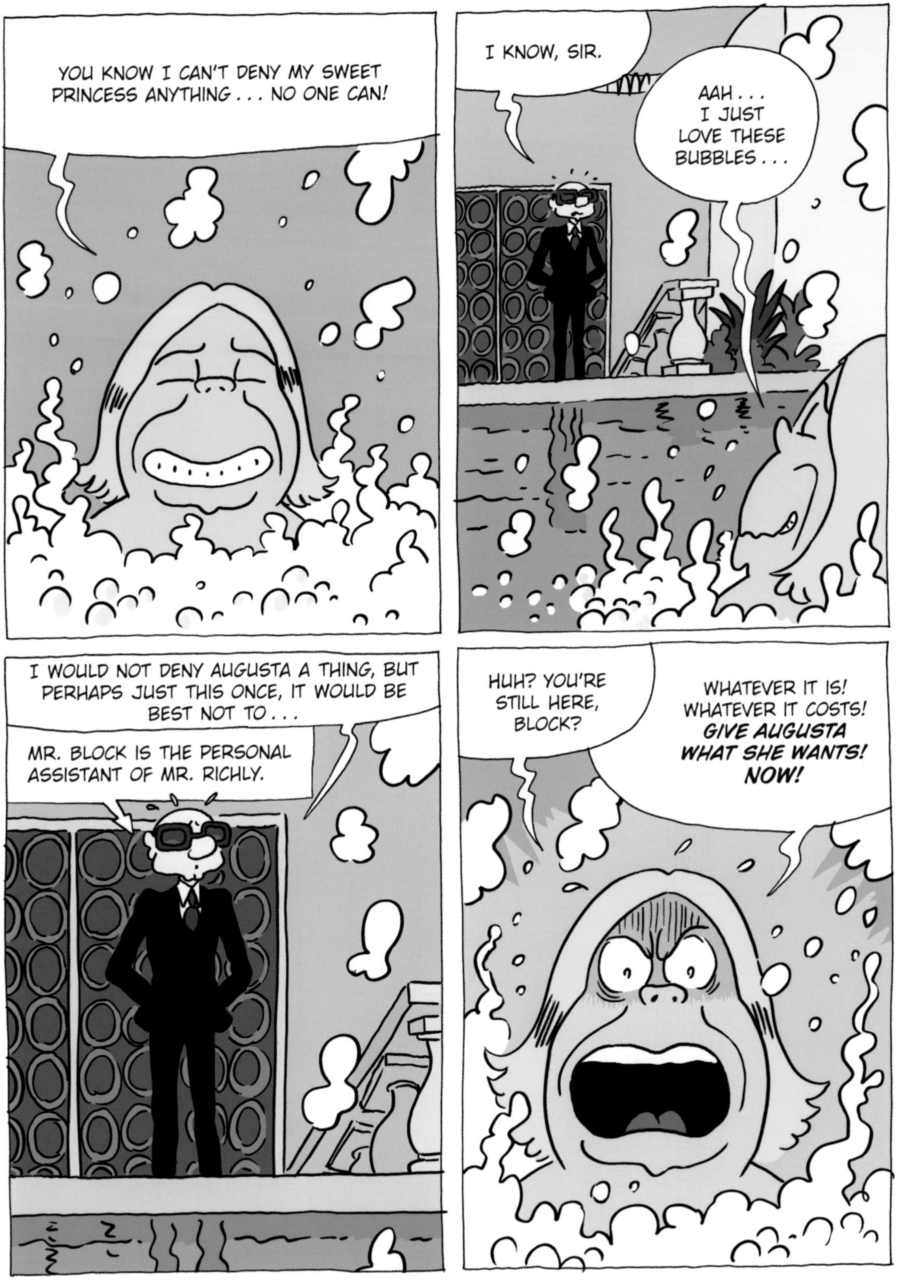
YOU KNOW I CAN'T DENY MY SWEET PRINCESS ANYTHING . . . NO ONE CAN!
I KNOW, SIR.
AAH . . . I JUST LOVE THESE BUBBLES . . .
I WOULD NOT DENY AUGUSTA A THING, BUT PERHAPS JUST THIS ONCE, IT WOULD BE BEST NOT TO . . .
MR. BLOCK IS THE PERSONAL ASSISTANT OF MR. RICHLY.
HUH? YOU'RE STILL HERE, BLOCK?
WHATEVER IT IS! WHATEVER IT COSTS! GIVE AUGUSTA WHAT SHE WANTS! NOW!

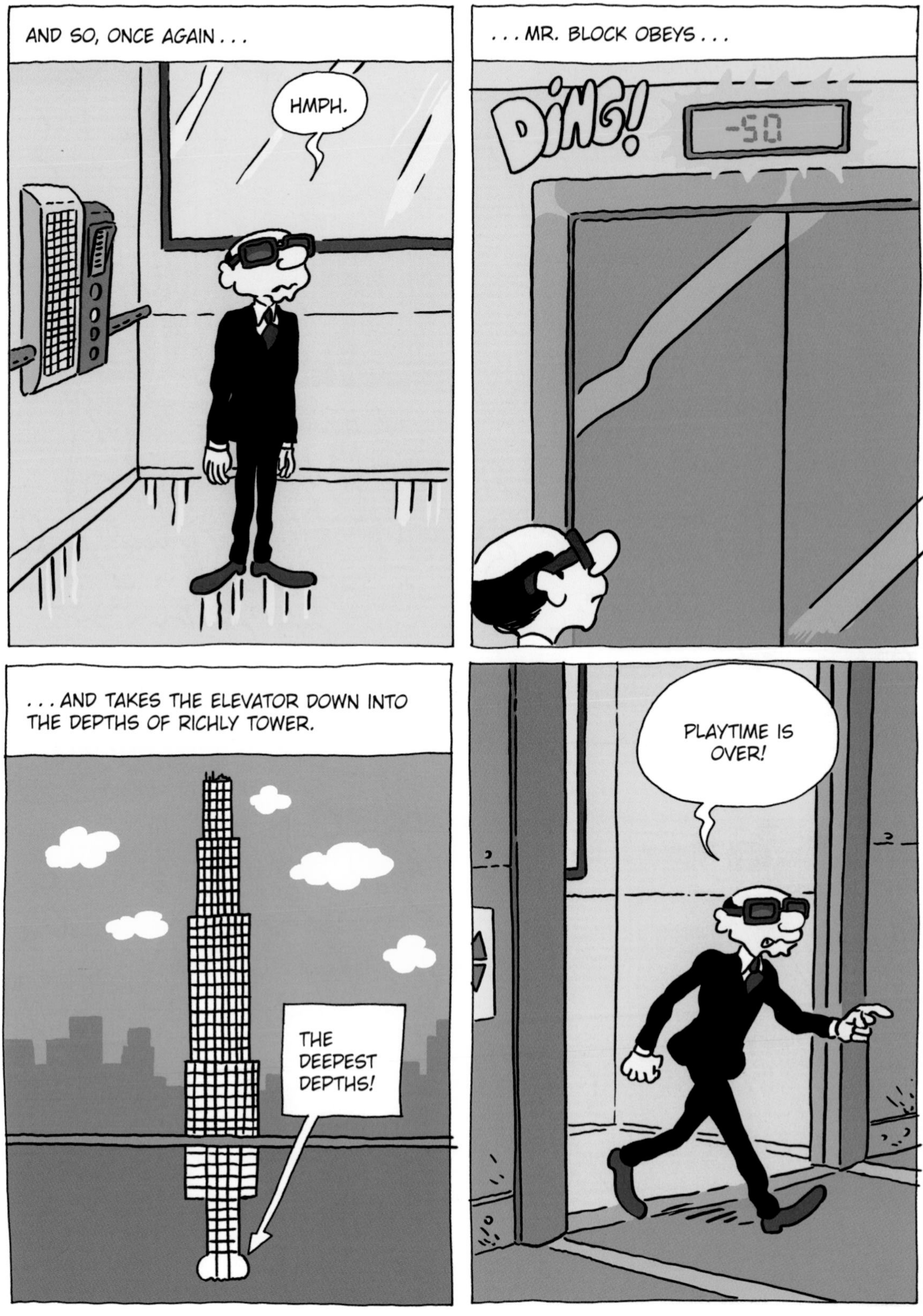
AND SO, ONCE AGAIN . . .
HMPH.
. . . MR. BLOCK OBEYS . . .
DING!
-50
. . . AND TAKES THE ELEVATOR DOWN INTO THE DEPTHS OF RICHLY TOWER.
THE DEEPEST DEPTHS!
PLAYTIME IS OVER!

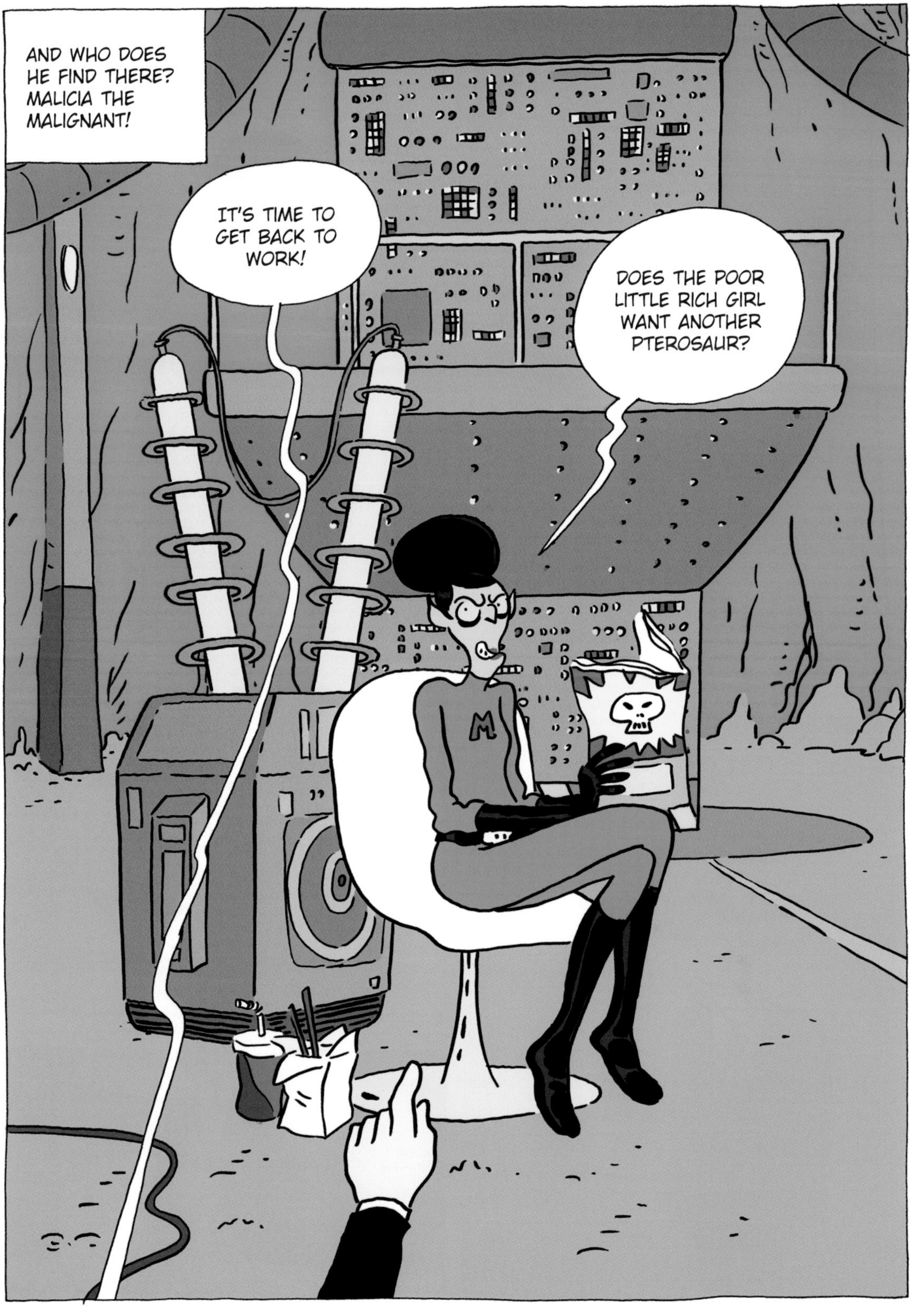
AND WHO DOES HE FIND THERE? MALICIA THE MALIGNANT!
IT'S TIME TO GET BACK TO WORK!
DOES THE POOR LITTLE RICH GIRL WANT ANOTHER PTEROSAUR?
M

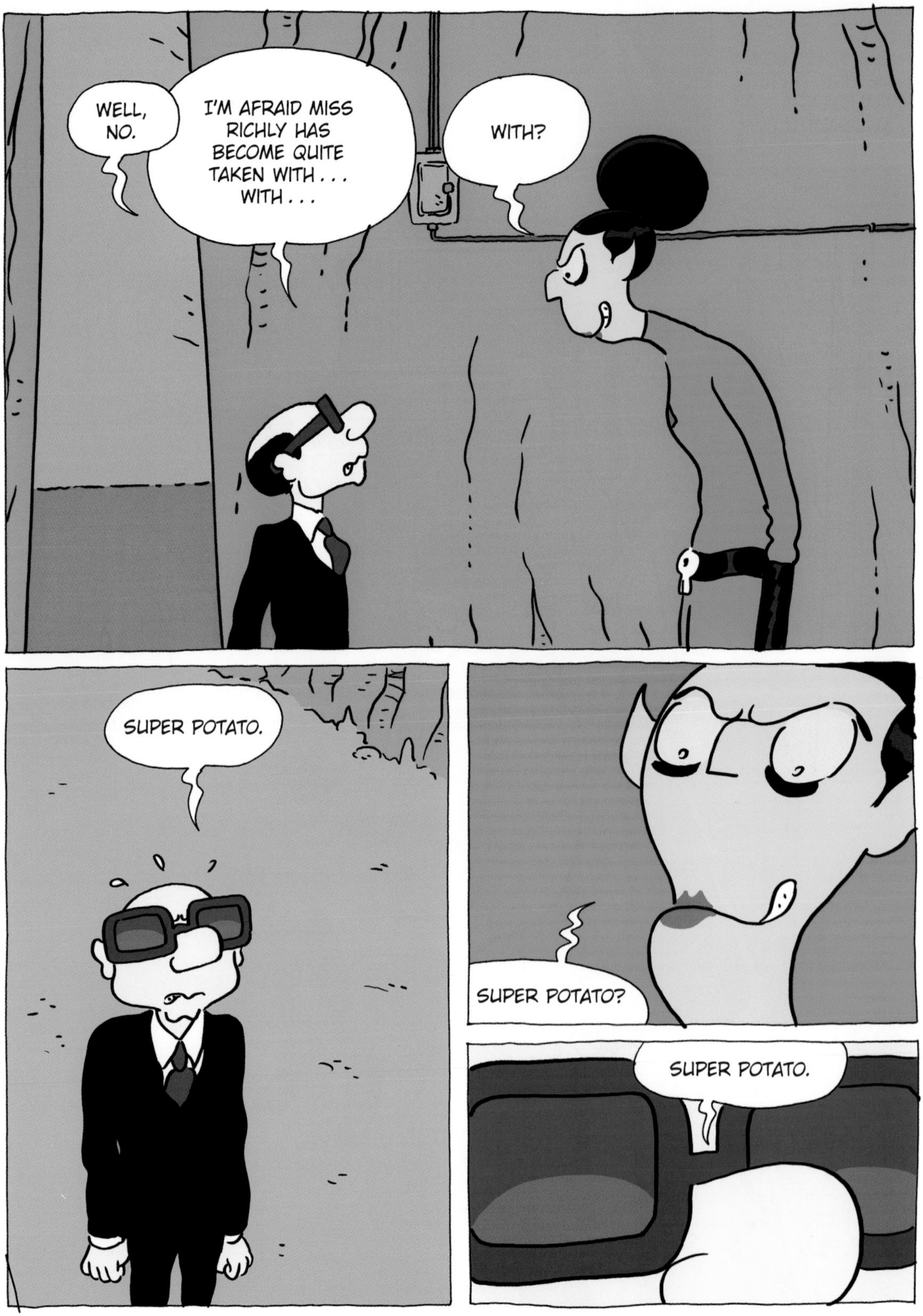
WELL, NO.
I'M AFRAID MISS RICHLY HAS BECOME QUITE TAKEN WITH . . . WITH . . .
WITH?
SUPER POTATO.
SUPER POTATO?
SUPER POTATO.

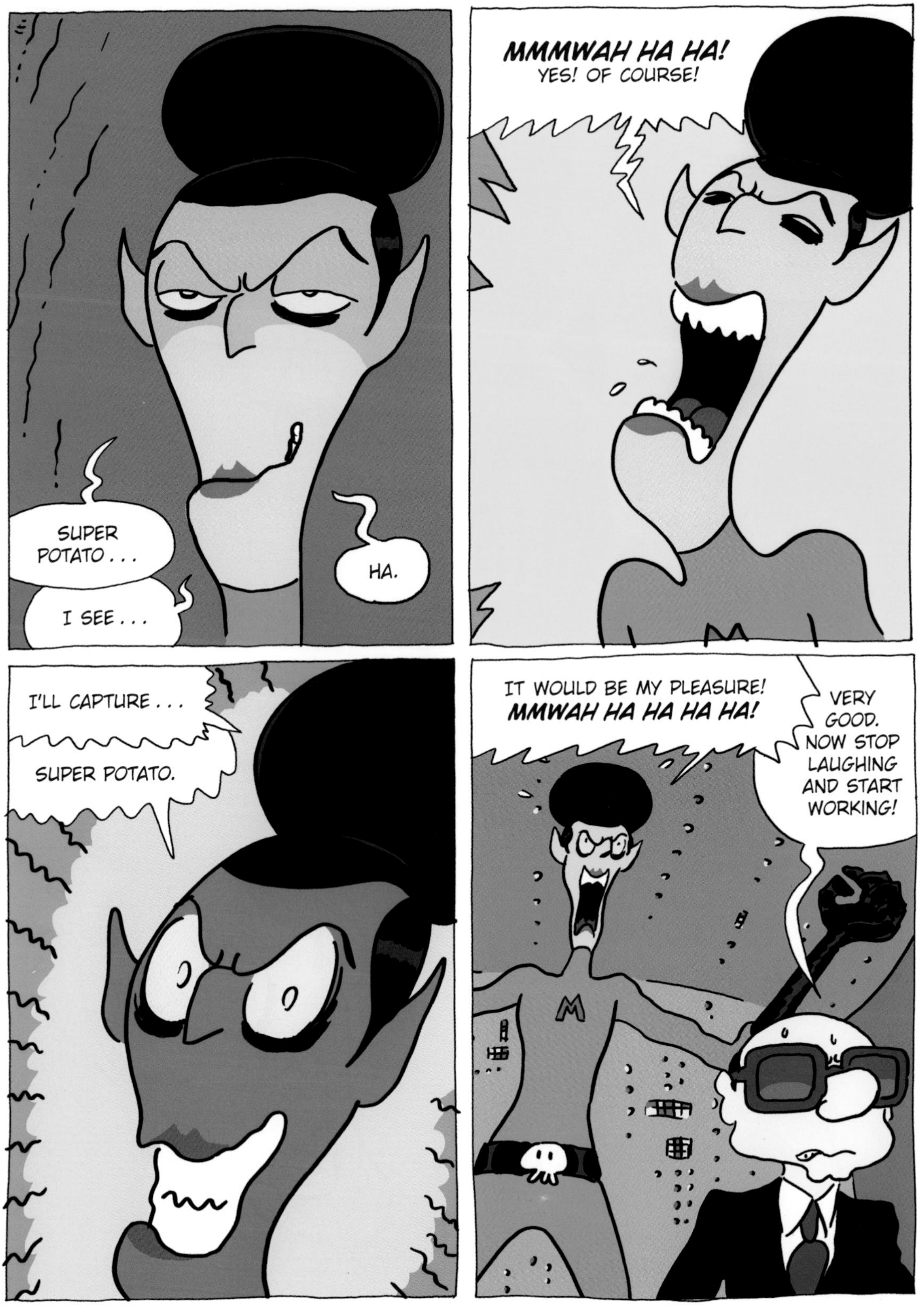
SUPER POTATO . . .
I SEE . . .
HA.
MMMWAH HA HA! YES! OF COURSE!
I'LL CAPTURE . . .
SUPER POTATO.
IT WOULD BE MY PLEASURE! MMWAH HA HA HA HA!
VERY GOOD. NOW STOP LAUGHING AND START WORKING!

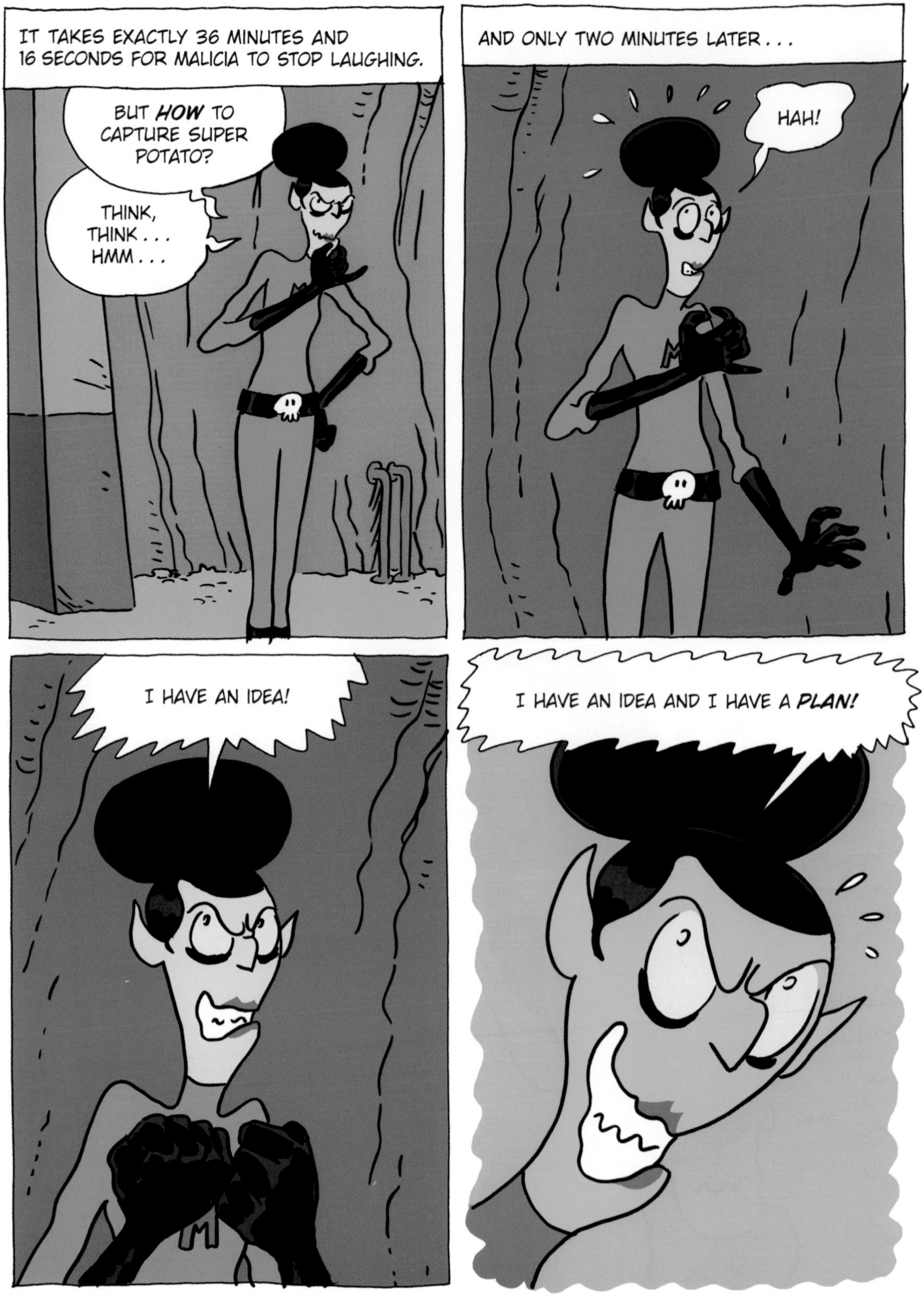
IT TAKES EXACTLY 36 MINUTES AND 16 SECONDS FOR MALICIA TO STOP LAUGHING.
BUT *HOW* TO CAPTURE SUPER POTATO?
THINK, THINK . . . HMM . . .
AND ONLY TWO MINUTES LATER . . .
HAH!
I HAVE AN IDEA!
I HAVE AN IDEA AND I HAVE A ***PLAN!***

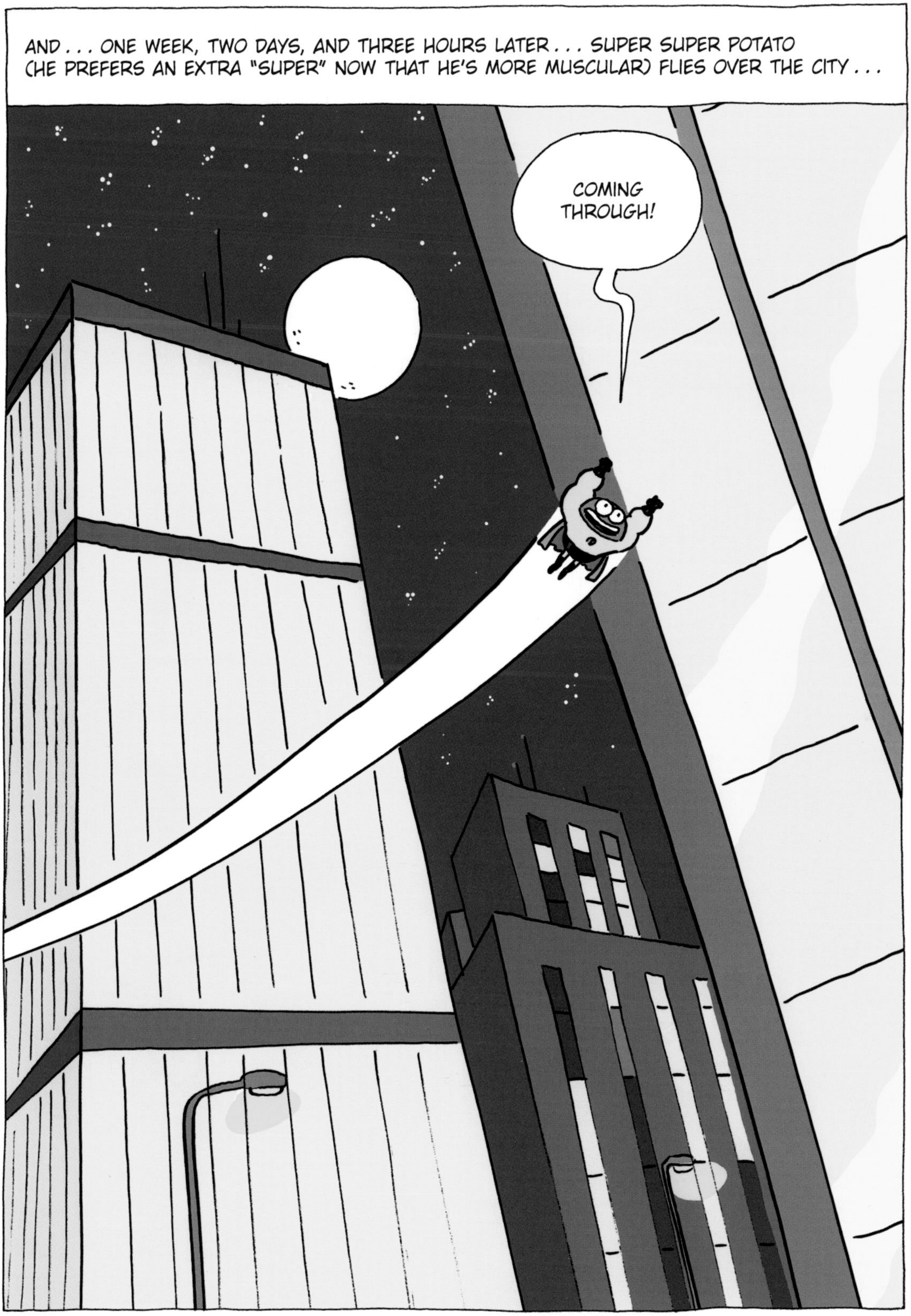
AND . . . ONE WEEK, TWO DAYS, AND THREE HOURS LATER . . . SUPER SUPER POTATO (HE PREFERS AN EXTRA "SUPER" NOW THAT HE'S MORE MUSCULAR) FLIES OVER THE CITY . . .
COMING THROUGH!

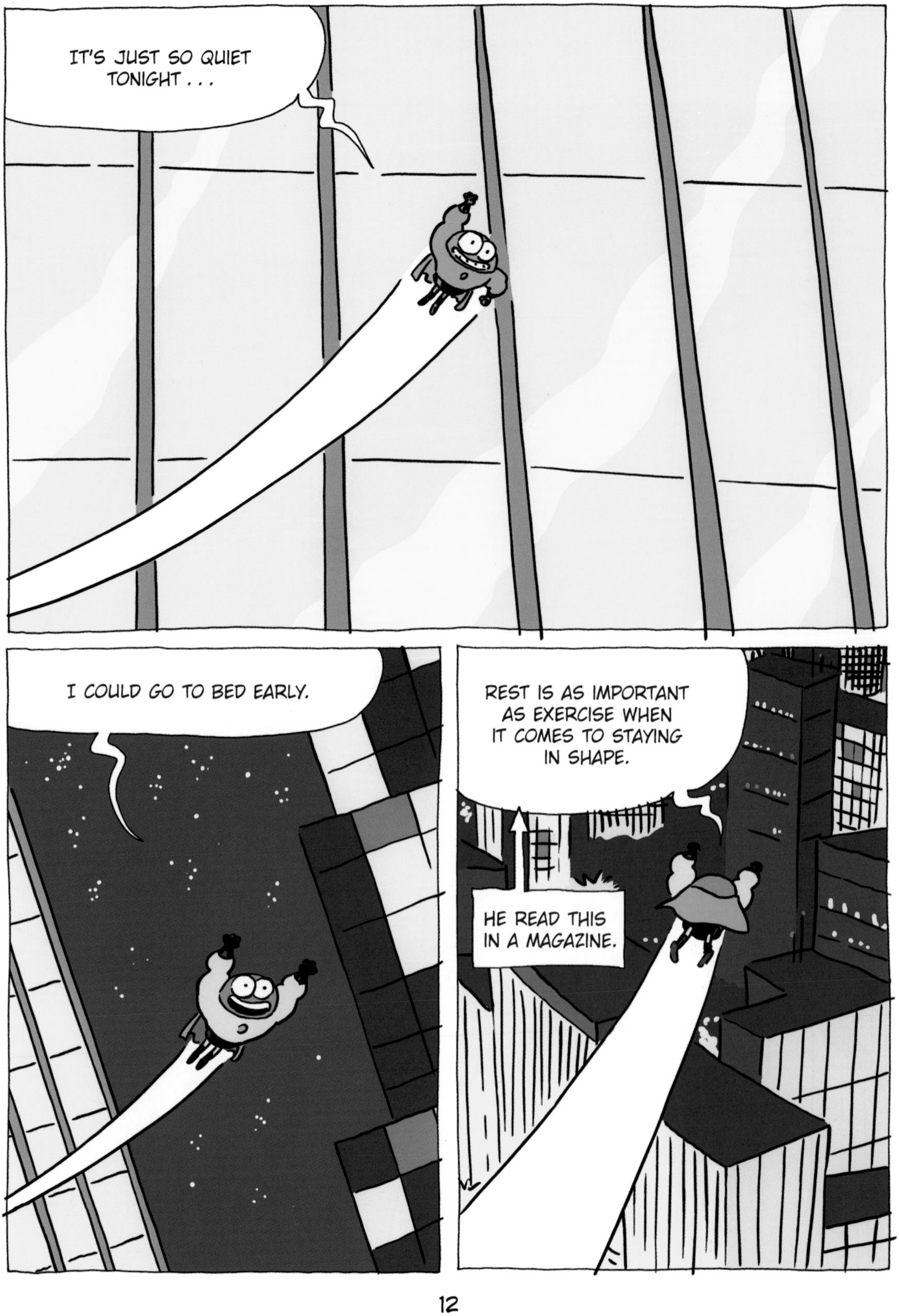
IT'S JUST SO QUIET TONIGHT . . .
I COULD GO TO BED EARLY.
REST IS AS IMPORTANT AS EXERCISE WHEN IT COMES TO STAYING IN SHAPE.
HE READ THIS IN A MAGAZINE.

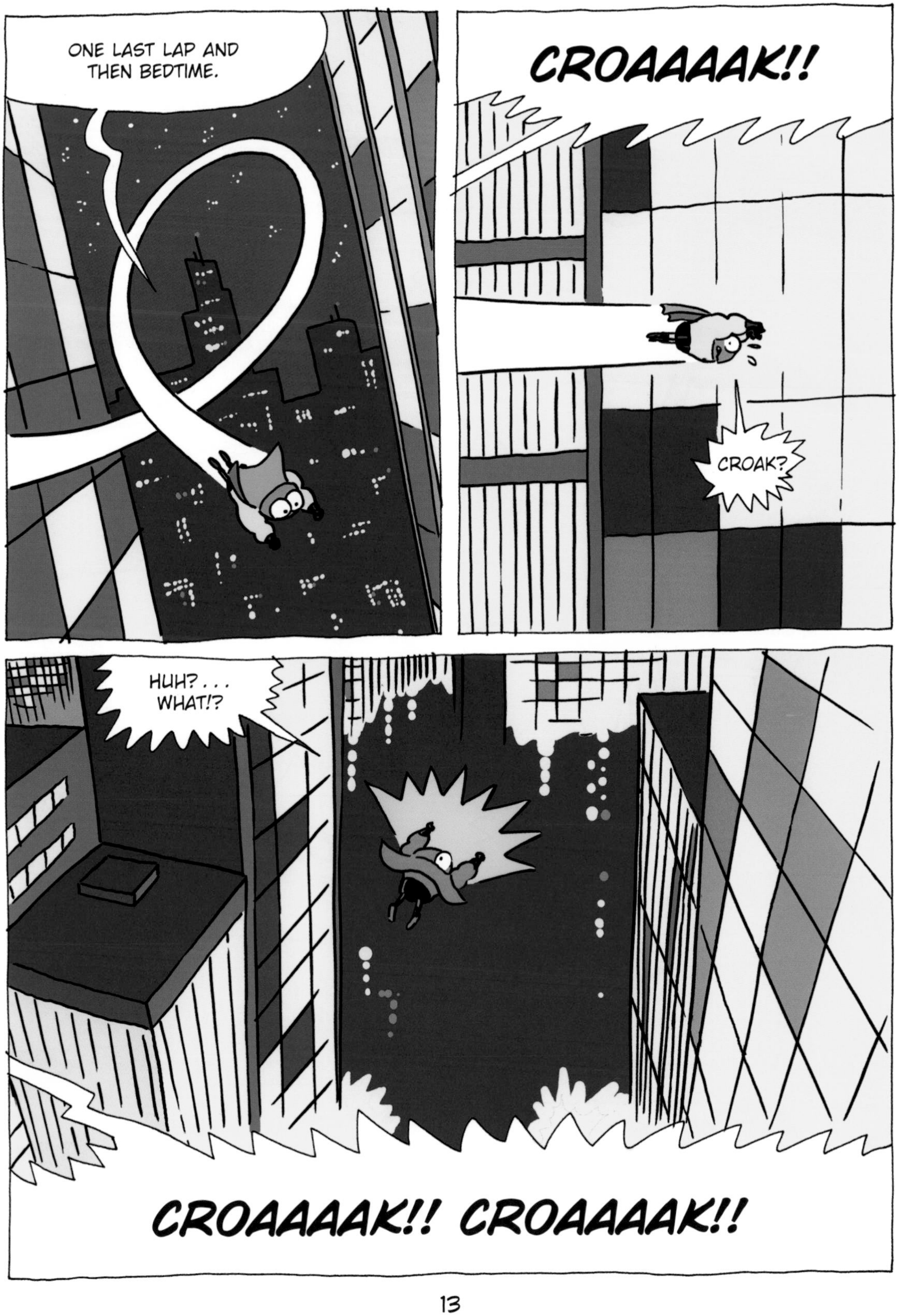
ONE LAST LAP AND THEN BEDTIME.
CROAAAAK!!
CROAK?
HUH? . . . WHAT!?
CROAAAAK!! CROAAAAK!!

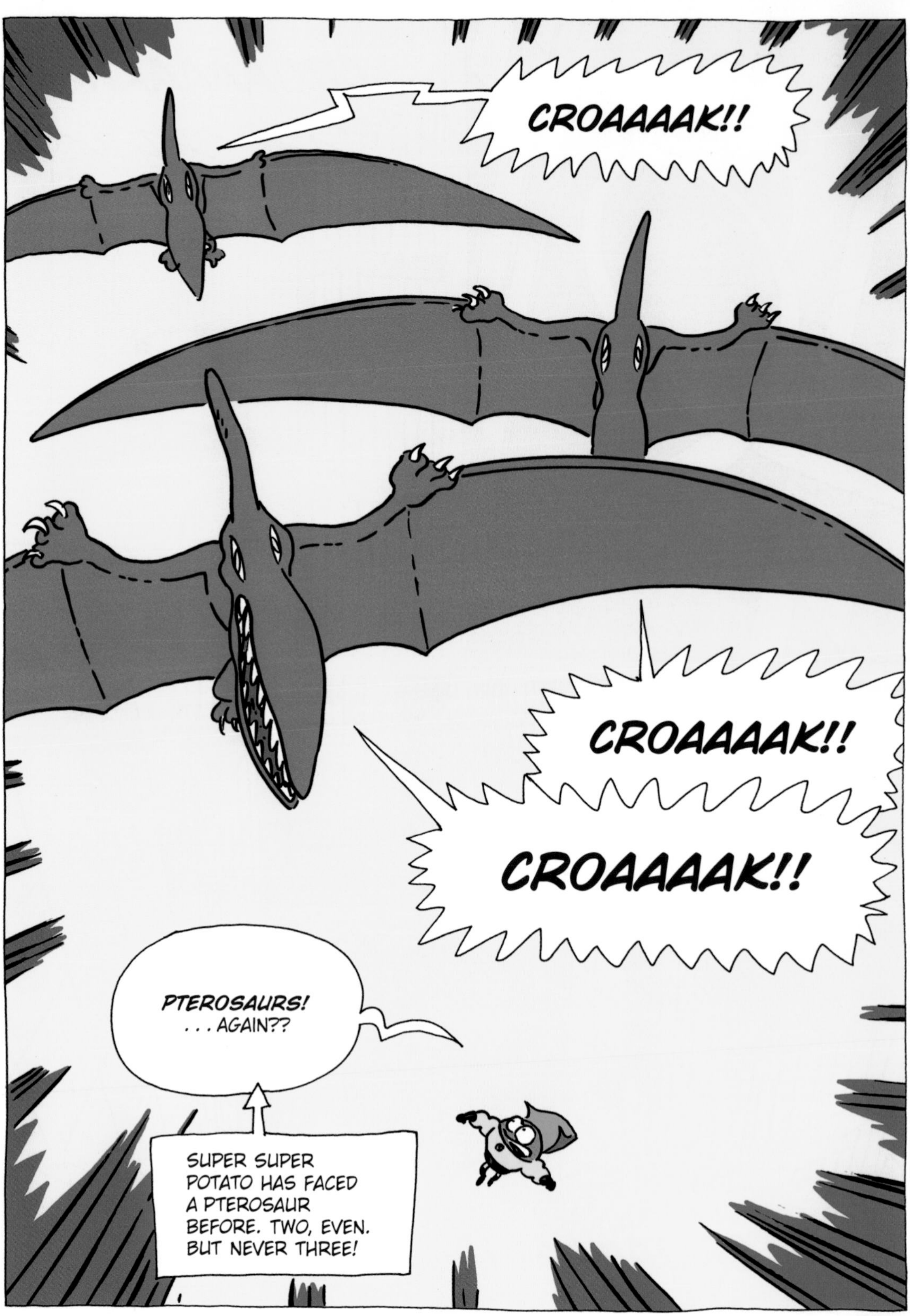
CROAAAAK!!
CROAAAAK!!
CROAAAAK!!
PTEROSAURS!
. . . AGAIN??
SUPER SUPER POTATO HAS FACED A PTEROSAUR BEFORE. TWO, EVEN. BUT NEVER THREE!

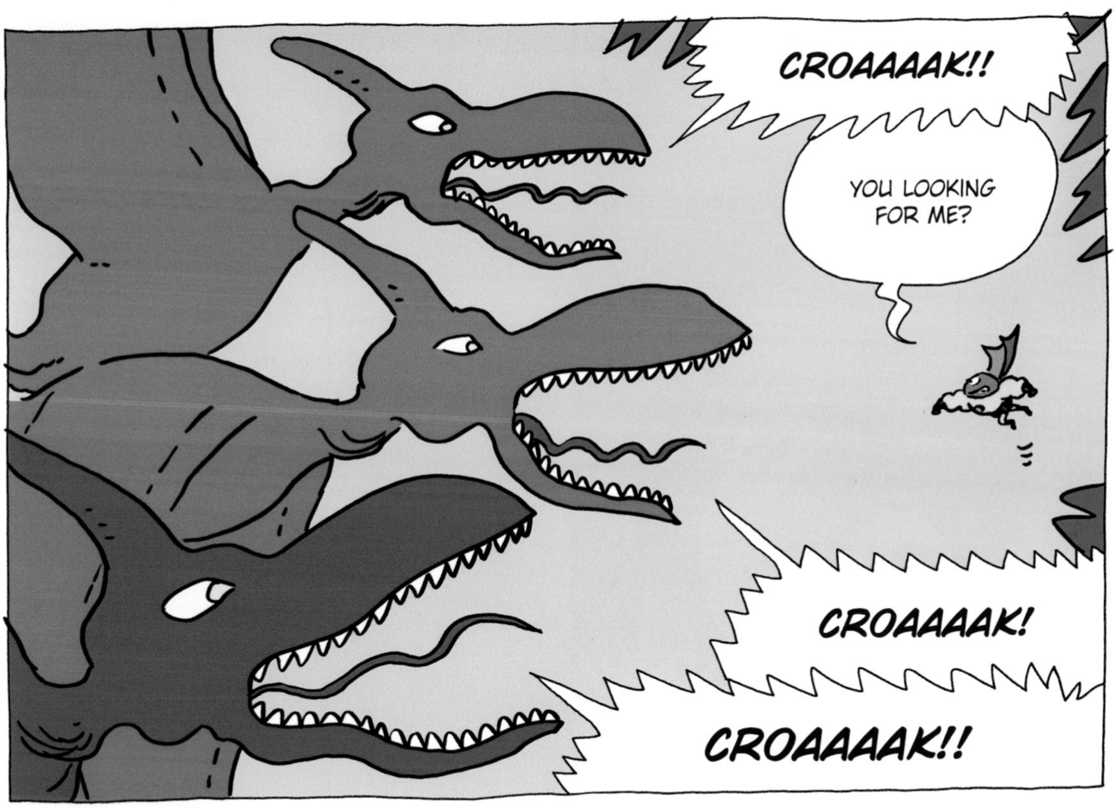
CROAAAAK!!
YOU LOOKING FOR ME?
CROAAAAK!
CROAAAAK!!

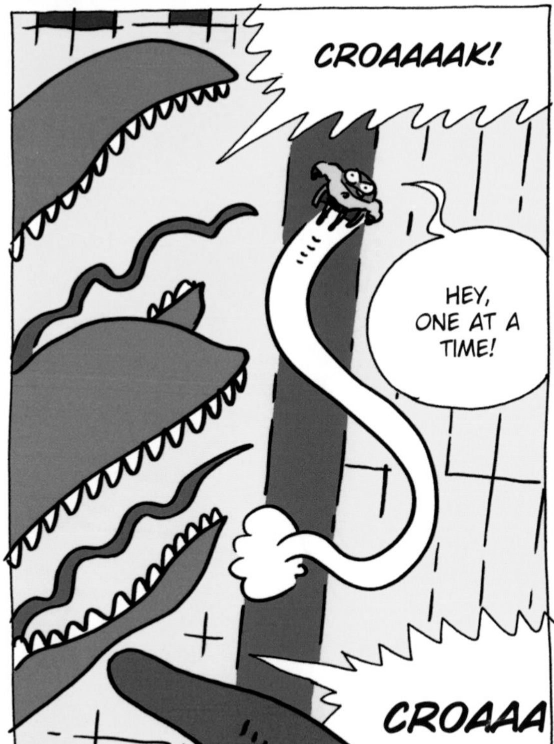
CROAAAAK!
HEY, ONE AT A TIME!
CROAAA

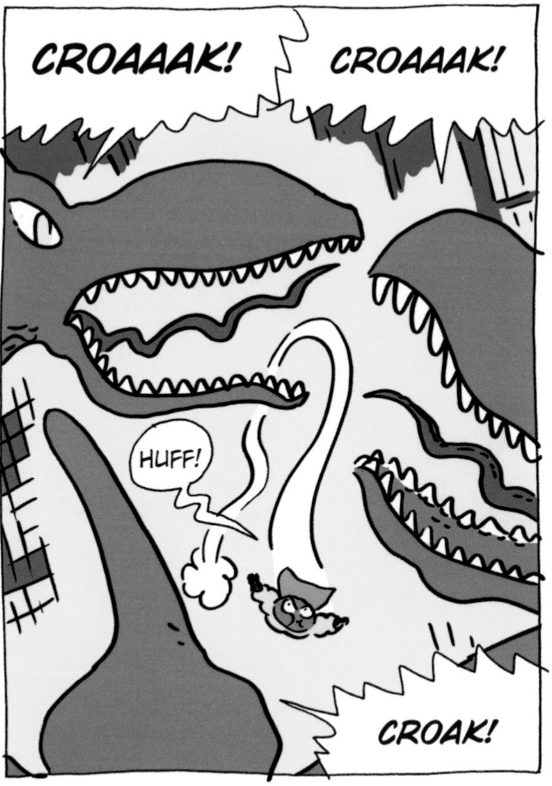
CROAAAK!
CROAAAK!
HUFF!
CROAK!

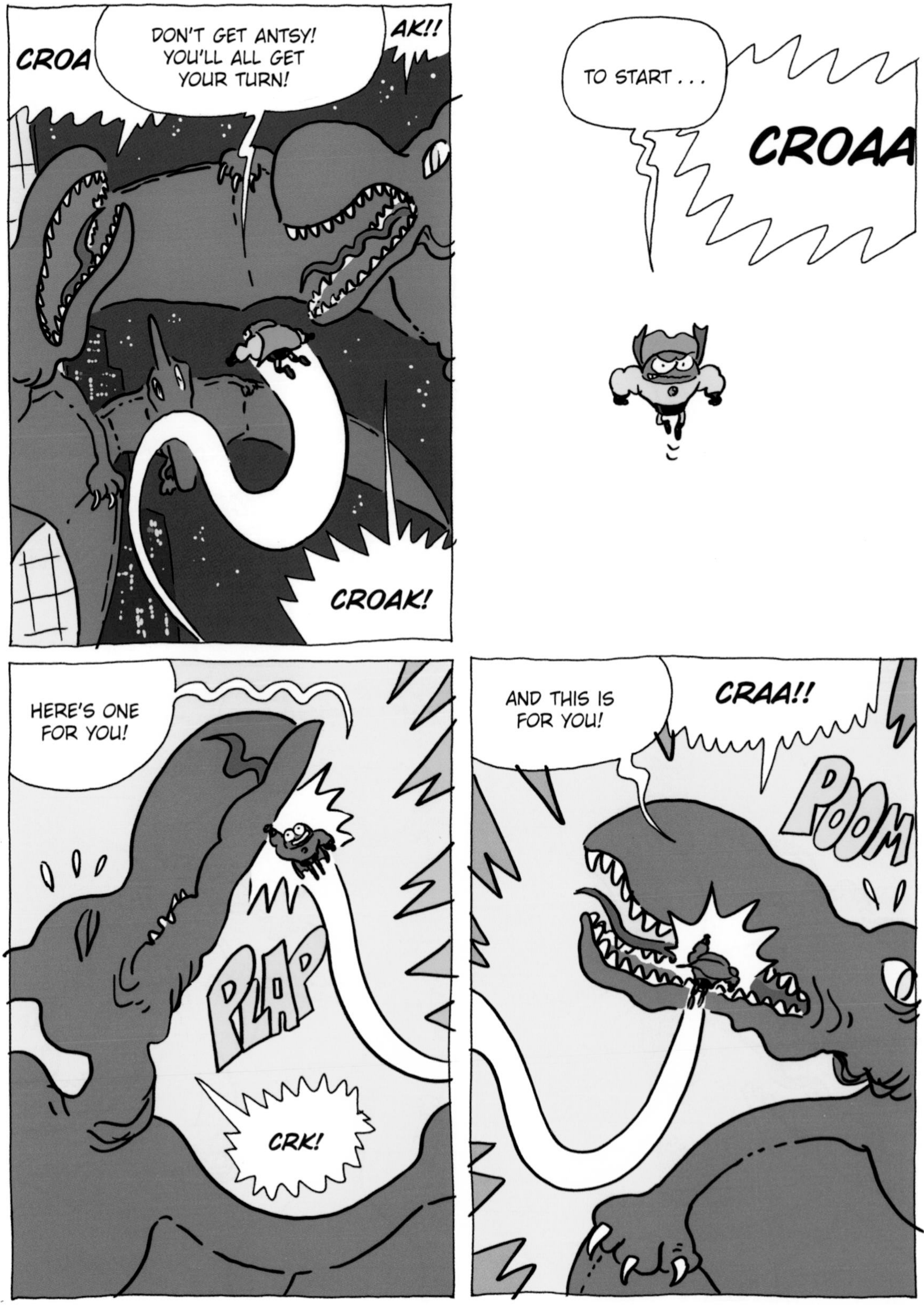
CROA
DON'T GET ANTSY! YOU'LL ALL GET YOUR TURN!
AK!!
CROAK!
TO START . . .
CROAA
HERE'S ONE FOR YOU!
PLAP
CRK!
AND THIS IS FOR YOU!
CRAA!!
POOM

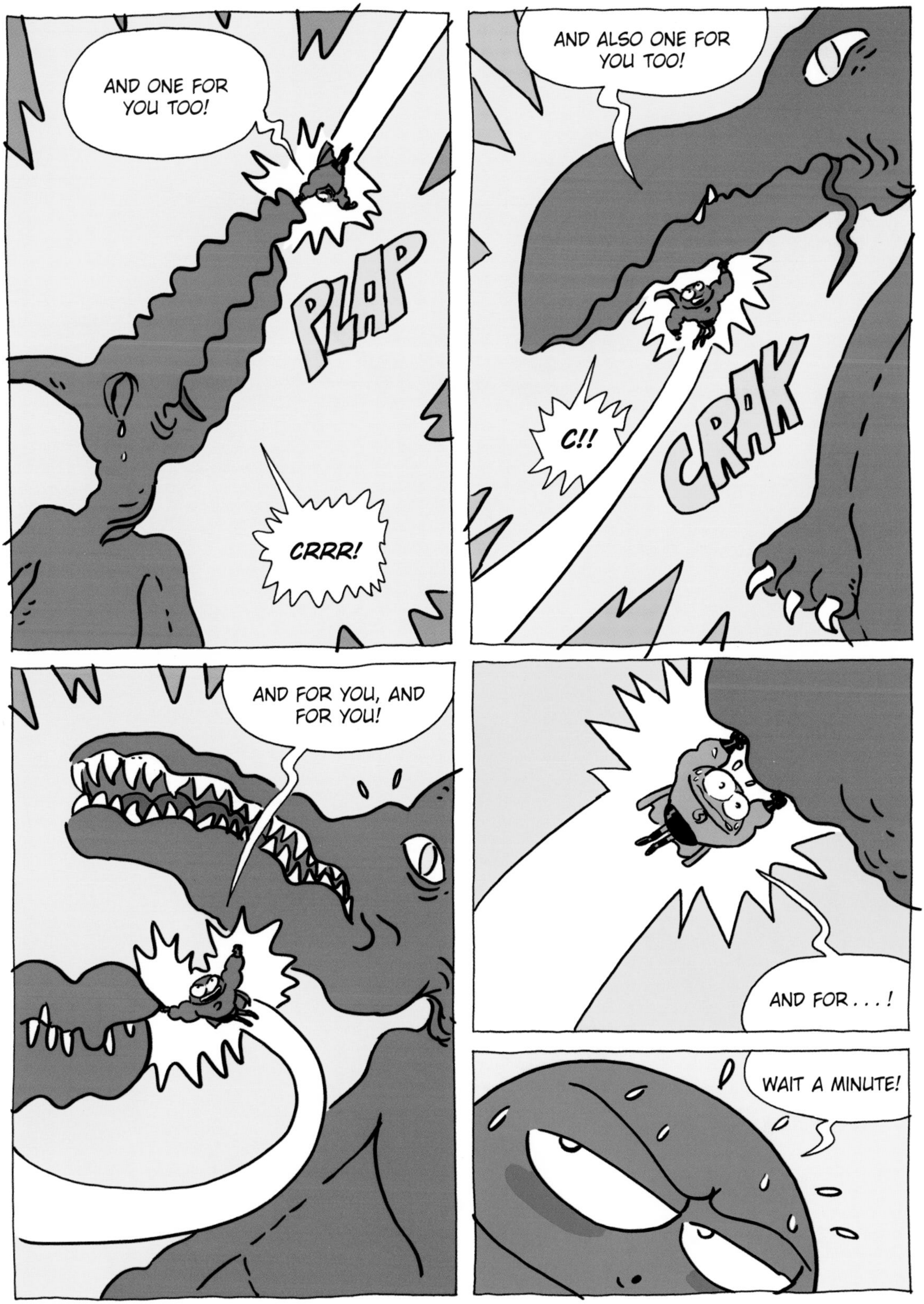
AND ONE FOR YOU TOO!
PLAP
CRRR!
AND ALSO ONE FOR YOU TOO!
C!!
CRAK
AND FOR YOU, AND FOR YOU!
AND FOR . . . !
WAIT A MINUTE!

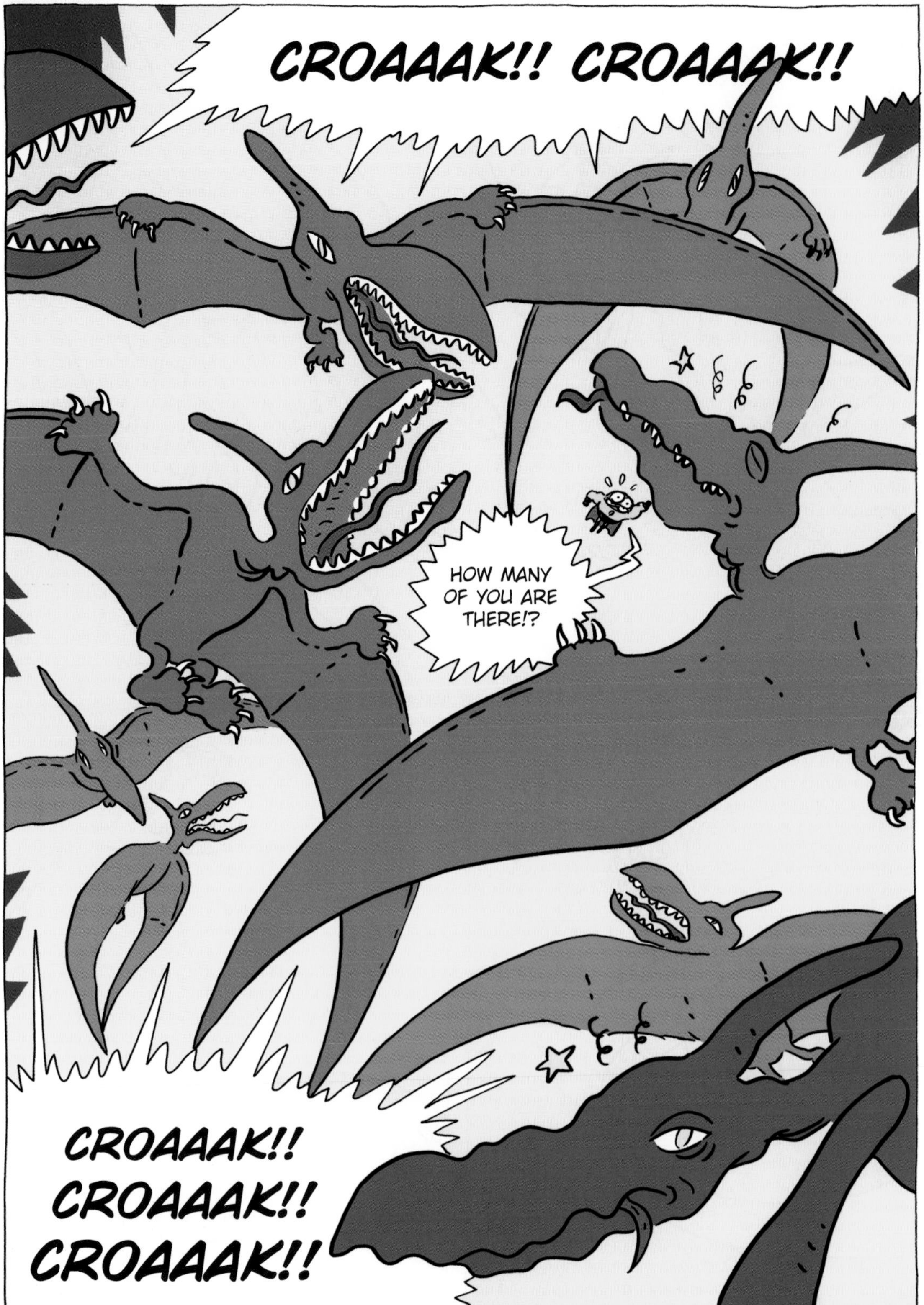
CROAAAK!! CROAAAK!!
HOW MANY OF YOU ARE THERE!?
CROAAAK!! CROAAAK!! CROAAAK!!

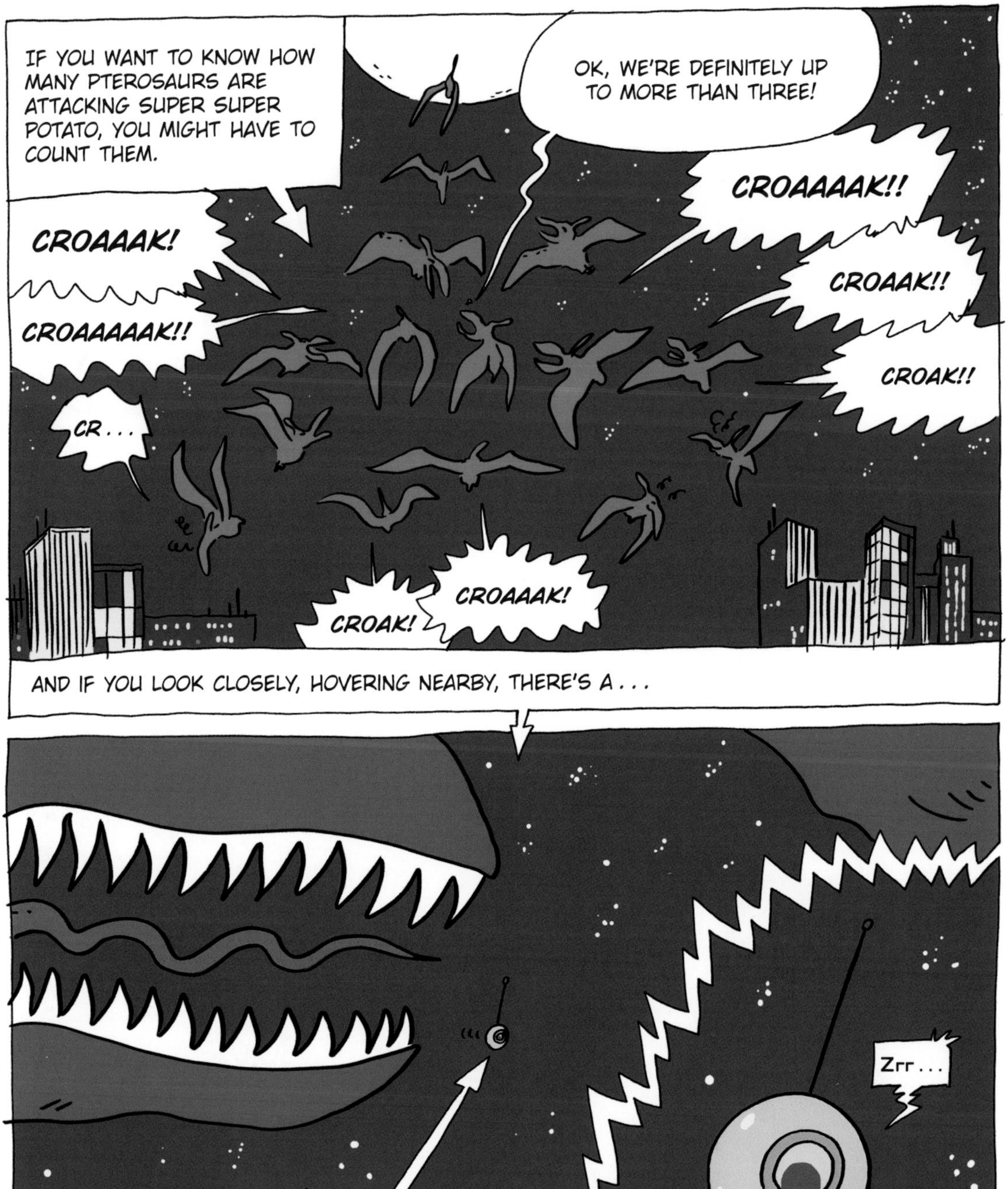

IF YOU WANT TO KNOW HOW MANY PTEROSAURS ARE ATTACKING SUPER SUPER POTATO, YOU MIGHT HAVE TO COUNT THEM.
OK, WE'RE DEFINITELY UP TO MORE THAN THREE!
CROAAAK!
CROAAAAAK!!
CROAAAAK!!
CROAAK!!
CROAK!!
CR . . .
CROAK!
CROAAAK!
AND IF YOU LOOK CLOSELY, HOVERING NEARBY, THERE'S A . . .
ROBOTIC MICRO-EYE!
Zrr . . .

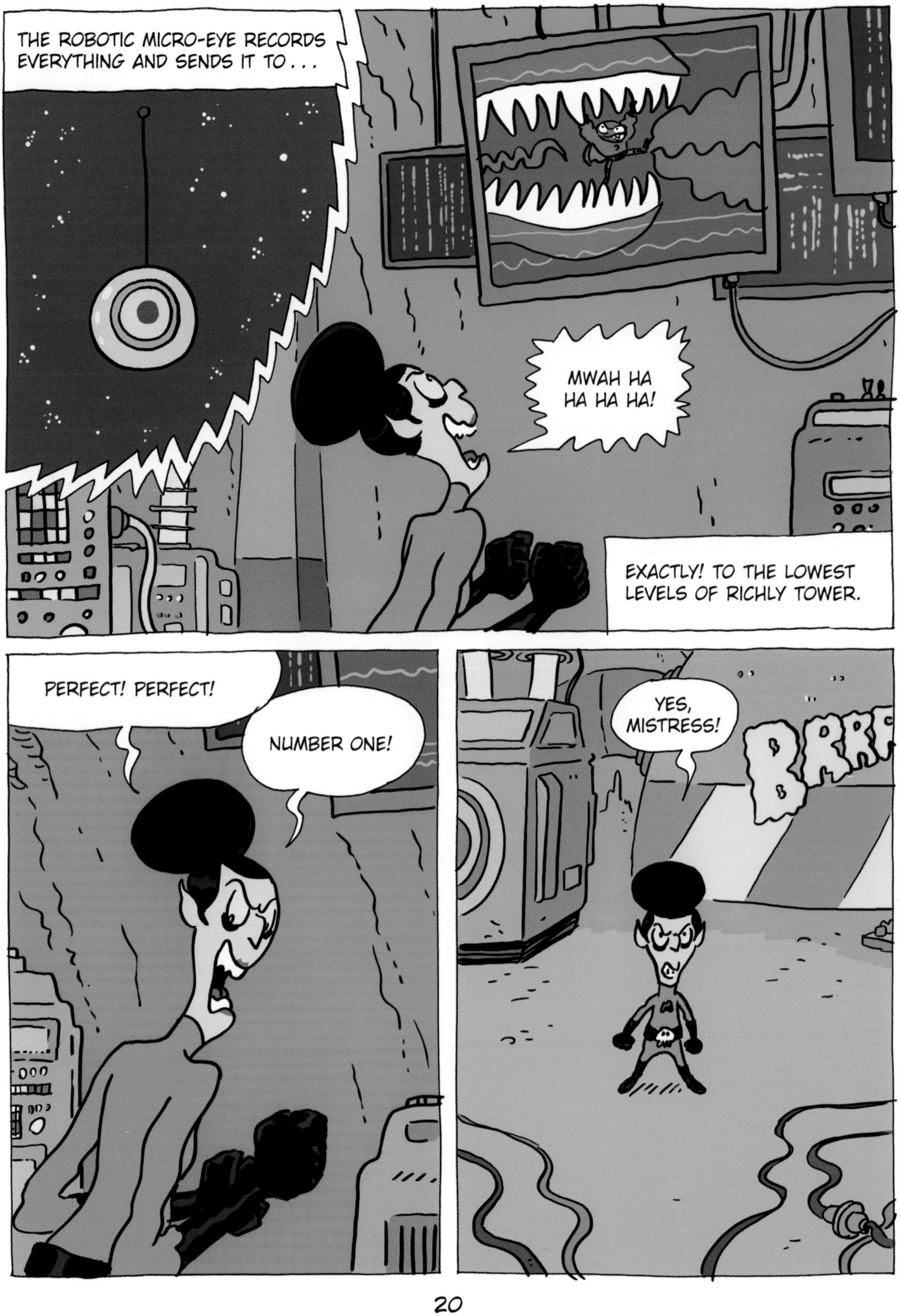
THE ROBOTIC MICRO-EYE RECORDS EVERYTHING AND SENDS IT TO . . .
MWAH HA HA HA HA!
EXACTLY! TO THE LOWEST LEVELS OF RICHLY TOWER.
PERFECT! PERFECT!
NUMBER ONE!
YES, MISTRESS!

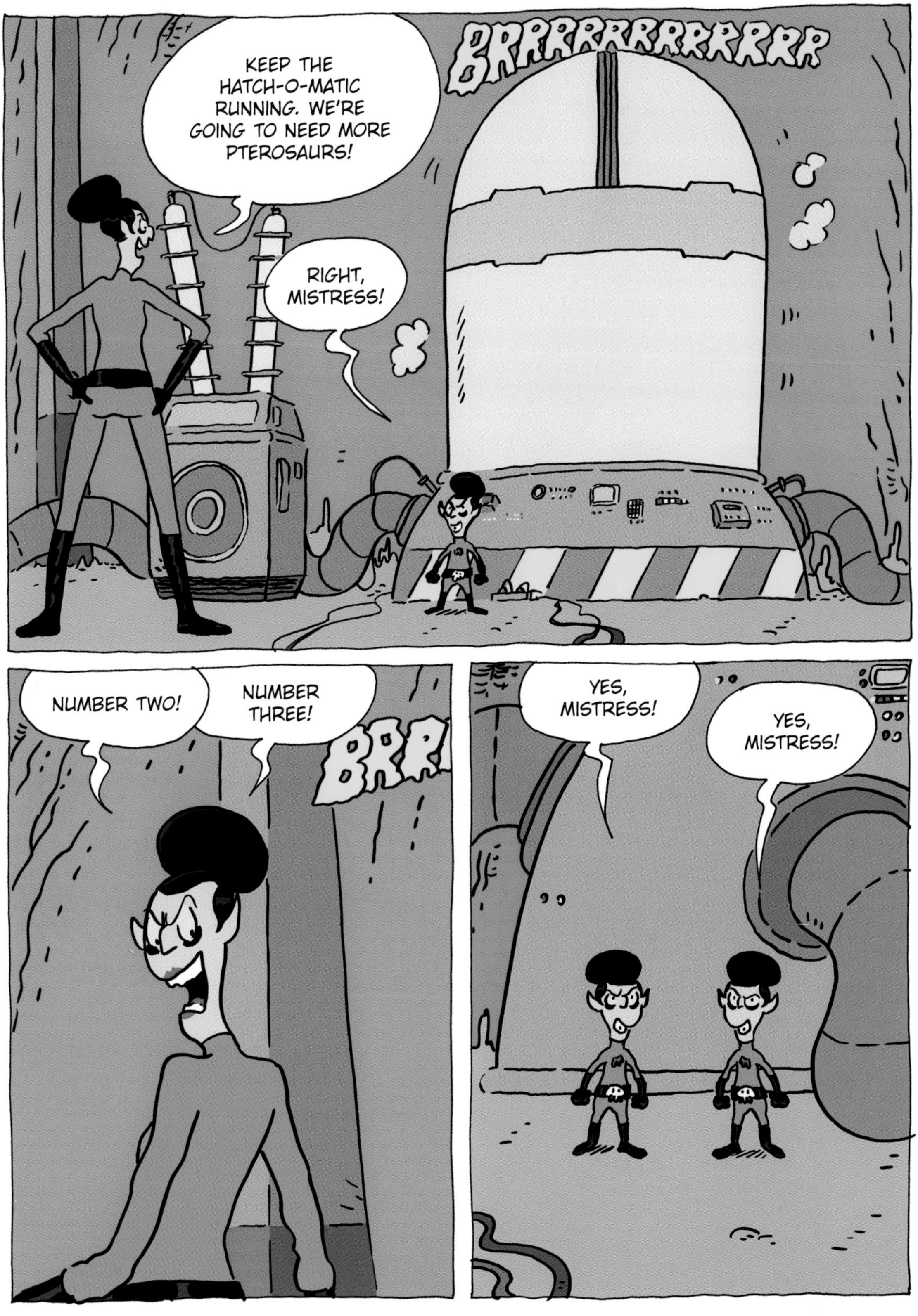
BRRRRRRRRRRRR
KEEP THE HATCH-O-MATIC RUNNING. WE'RE GOING TO NEED MORE PTEROSAURS!
RIGHT, MISTRESS!
NUMBER TWO!
NUMBER THREE!
BRR
YES, MISTRESS!
YES, MISTRESS!

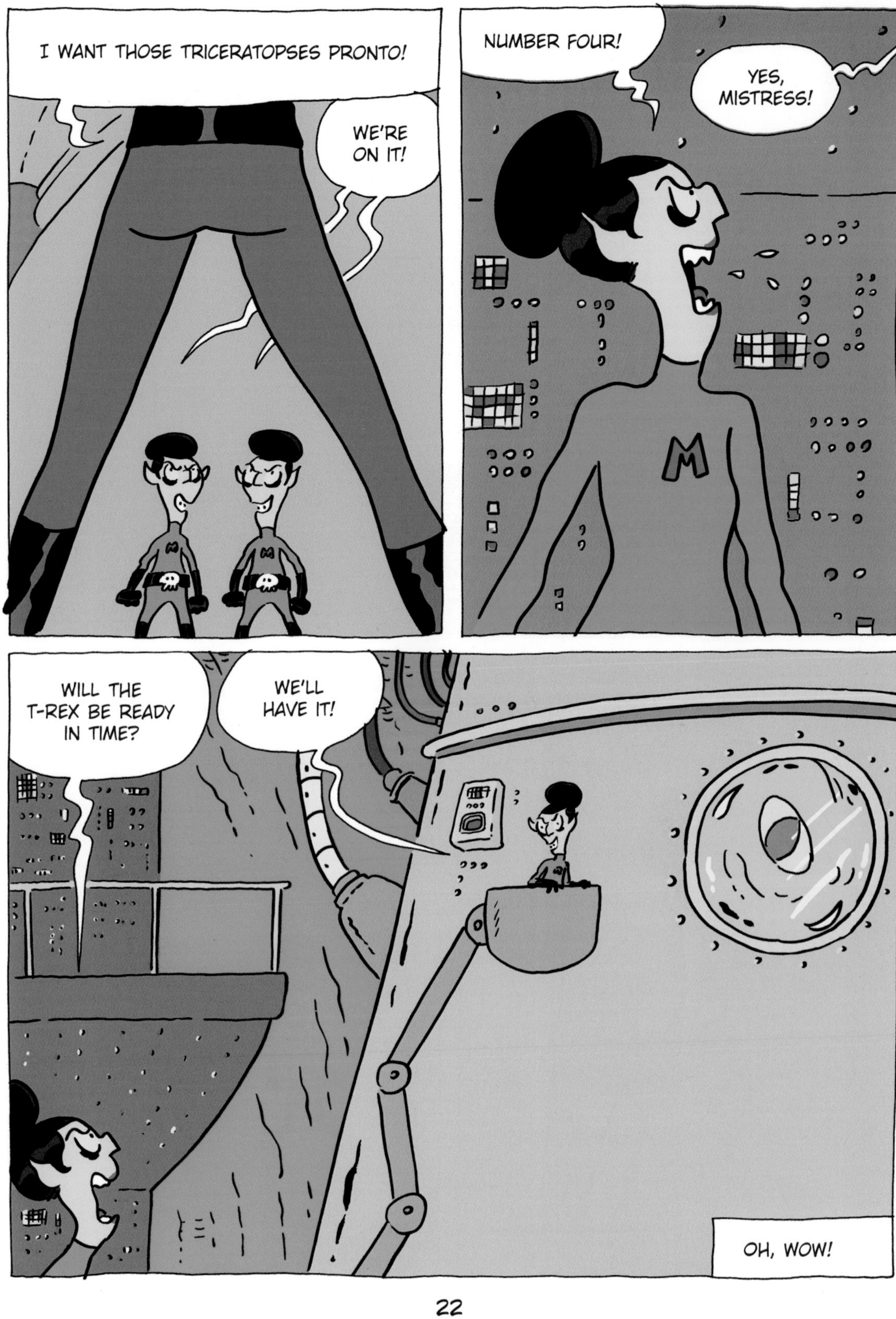
I WANT THOSE TRICERATOPSES PRONTO!
WE'RE ON IT!
NUMBER FOUR!
YES, MISTRESS!
WILL THE T-REX BE READY IN TIME?
WE'LL HAVE IT!
OH, WOW!

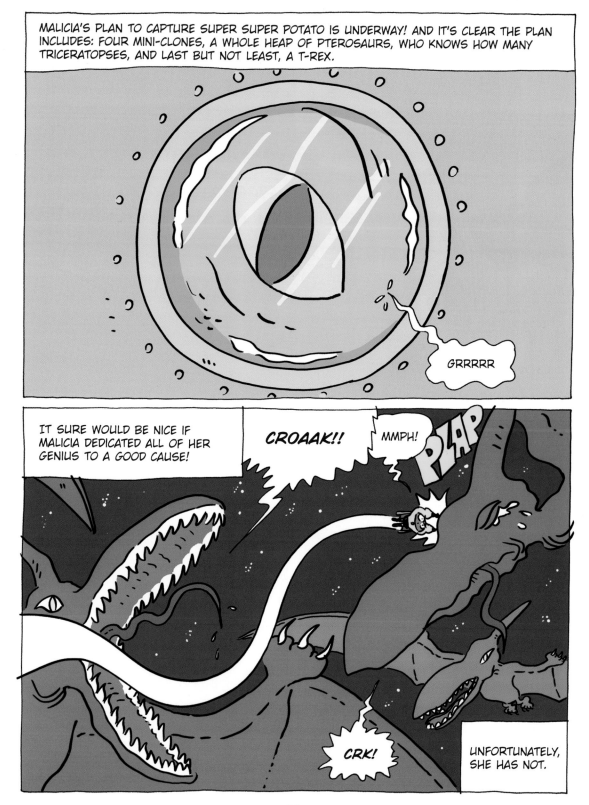

23

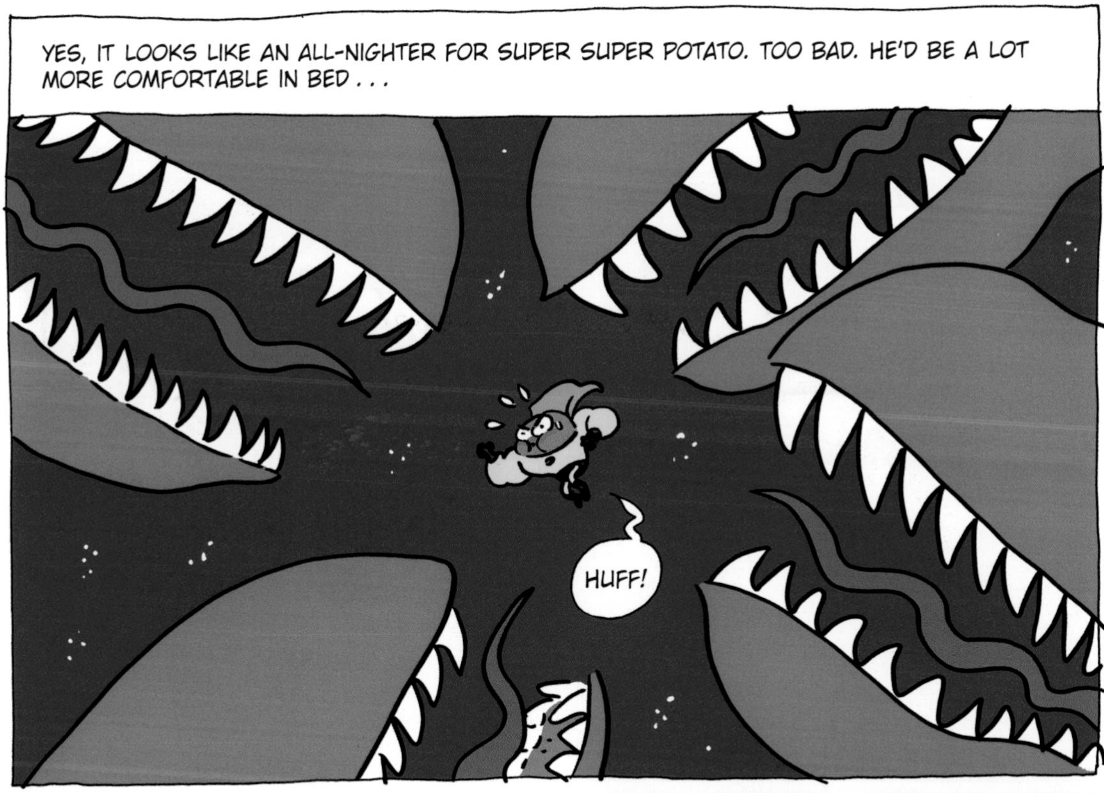
YES, IT LOOKS LIKE AN ALL-NIGHTER FOR SUPER SUPER POTATO. TOO BAD. HE'D BE A LOT MORE COMFORTABLE IN BED . . .
HUFF!

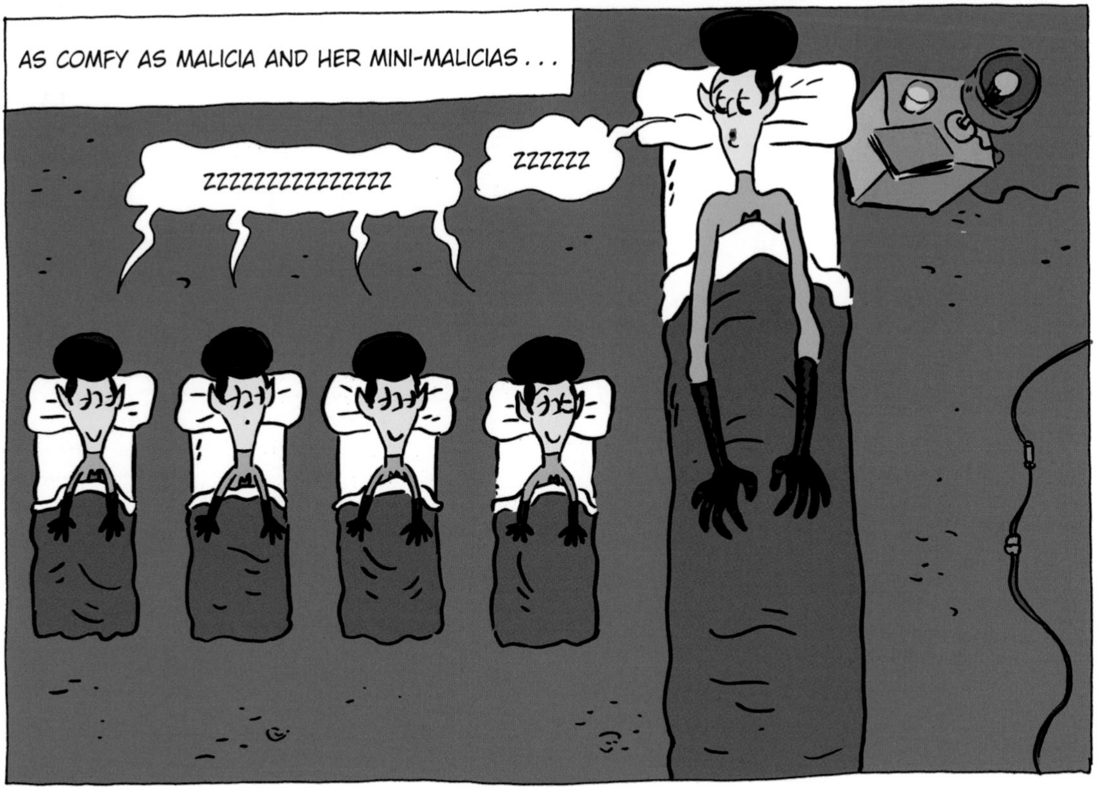
AS COMFY AS MALICIA AND HER MINI-MALICIAS . . .
ZZZZZZZZZZZZZZZZ
ZZZZZZ

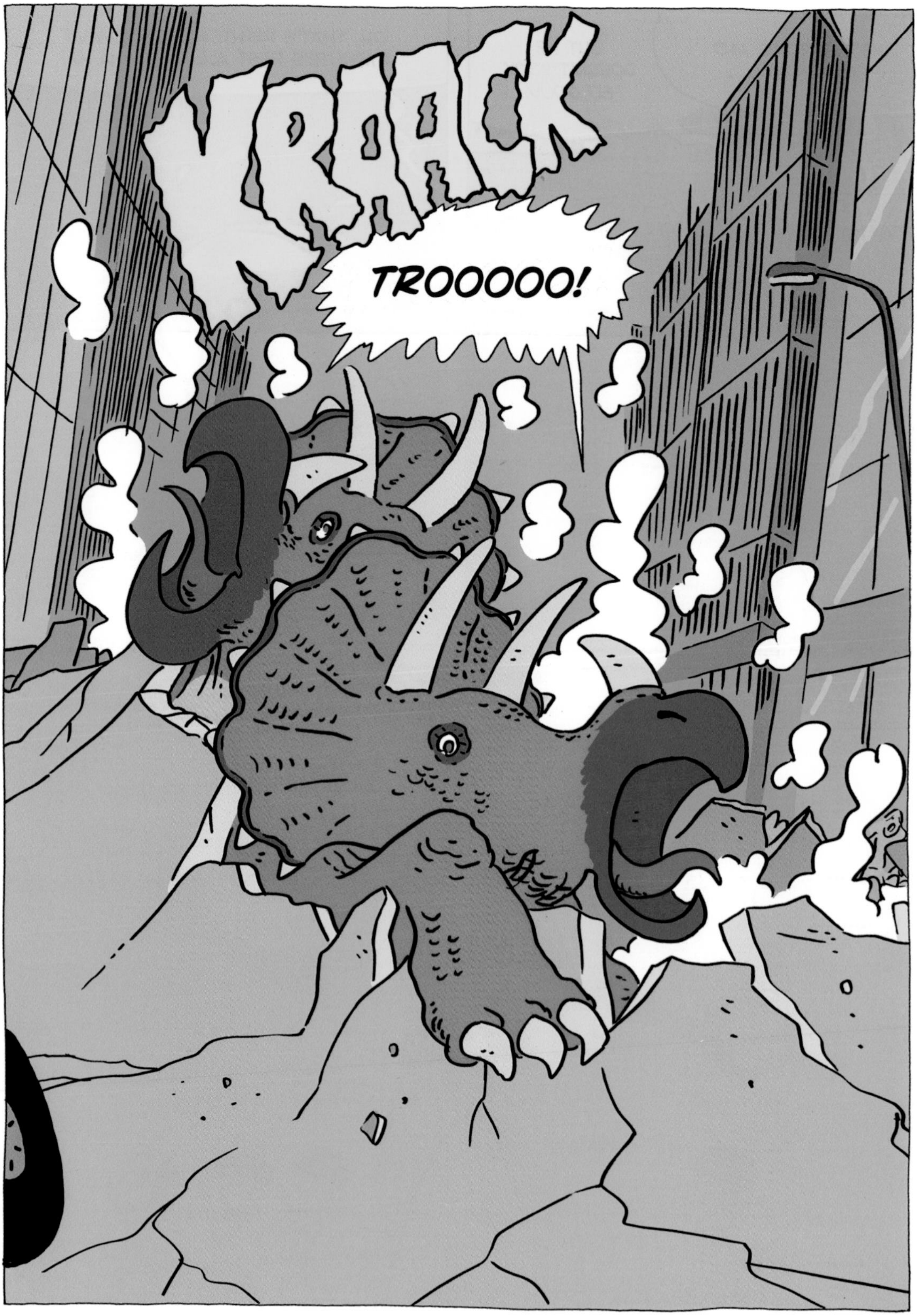
KRAACK
TROOOOO!

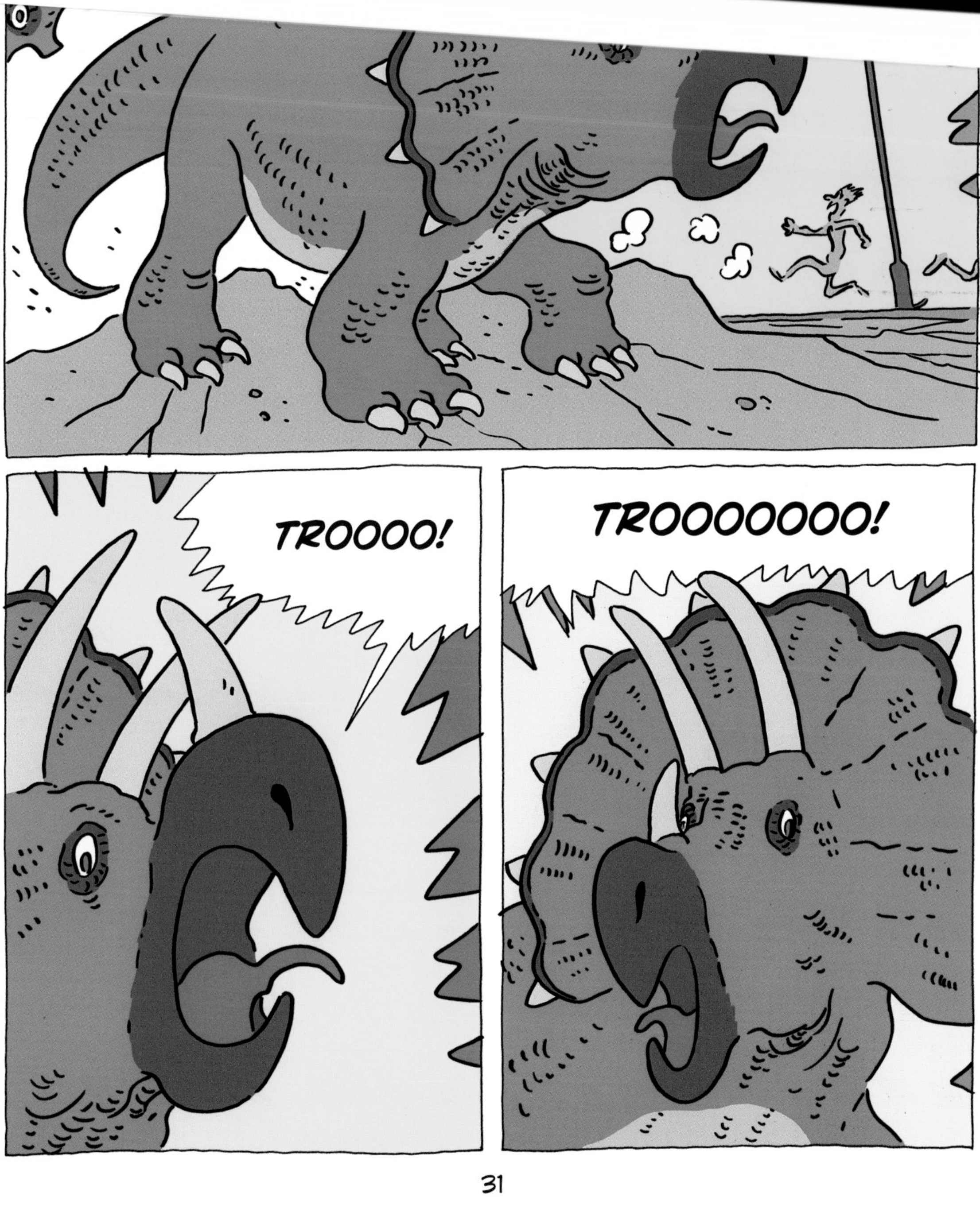
TROOOO!
TROOOOOOOO!

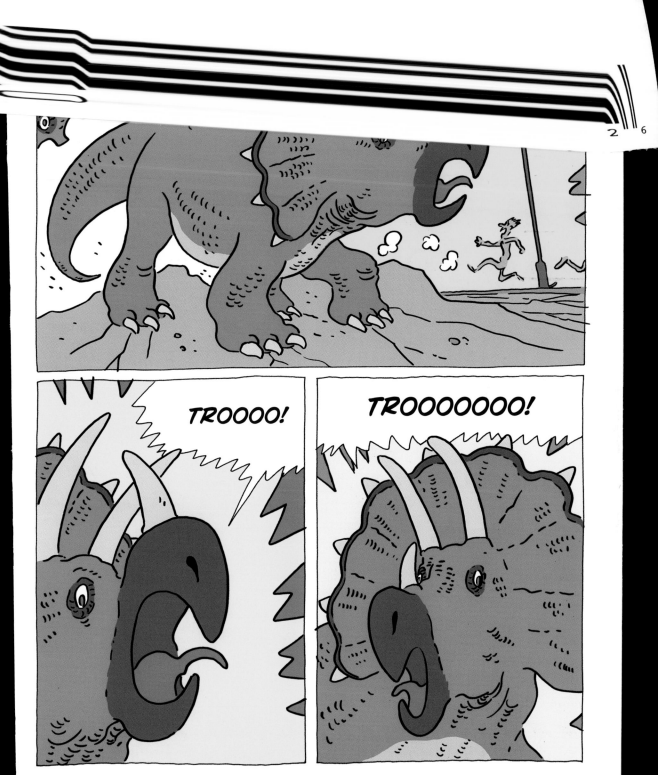

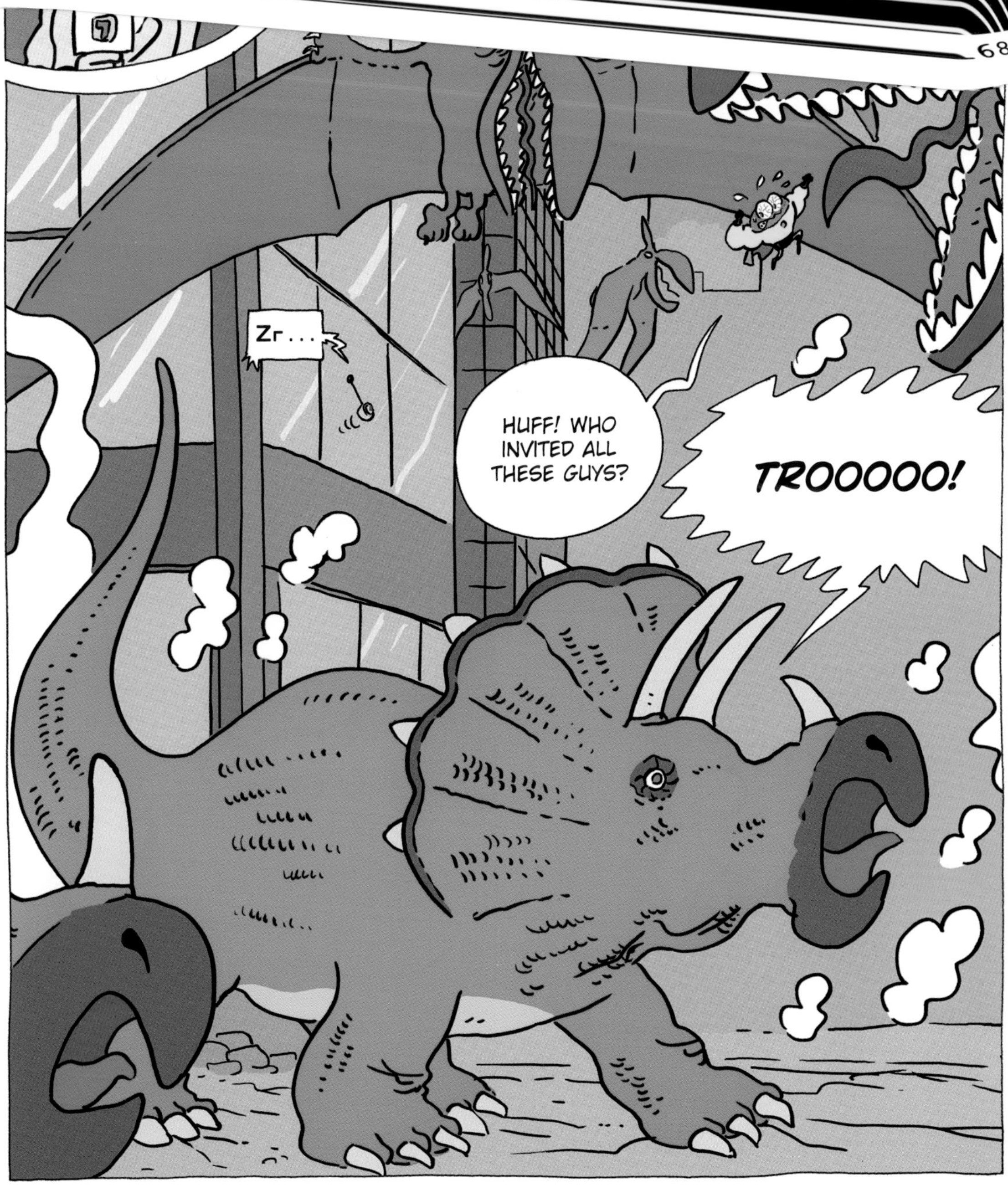
7
Zr . . .
HUFF! WHO INVITED ALL THESE GUYS?
TROOOOO!

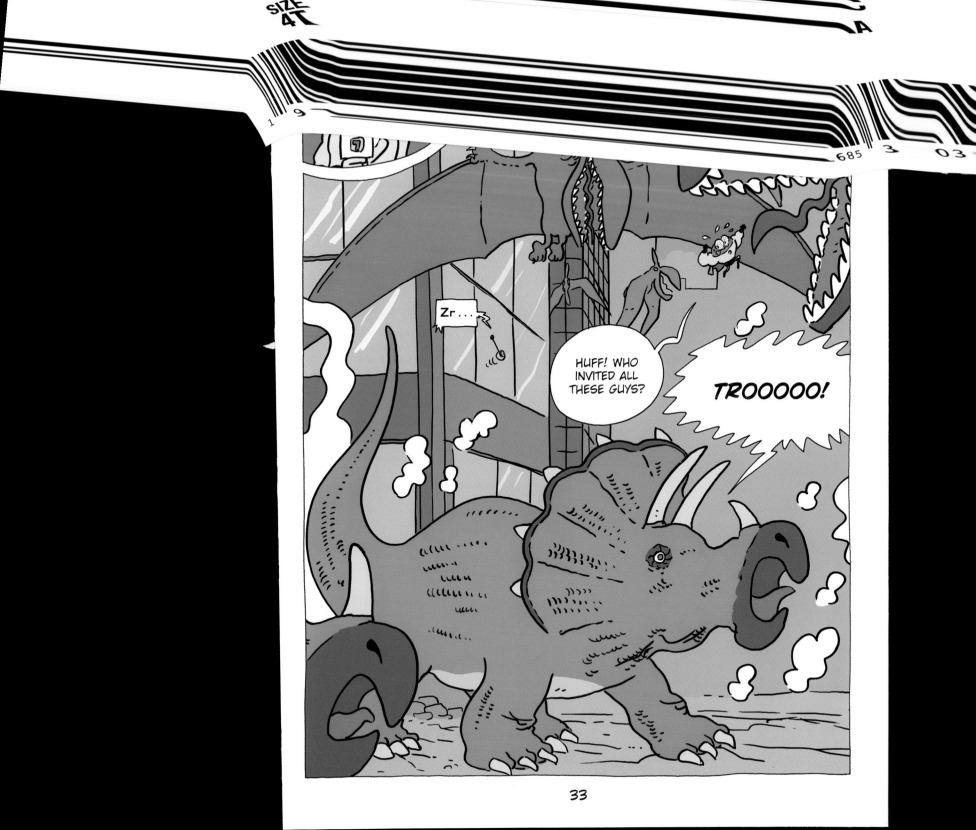

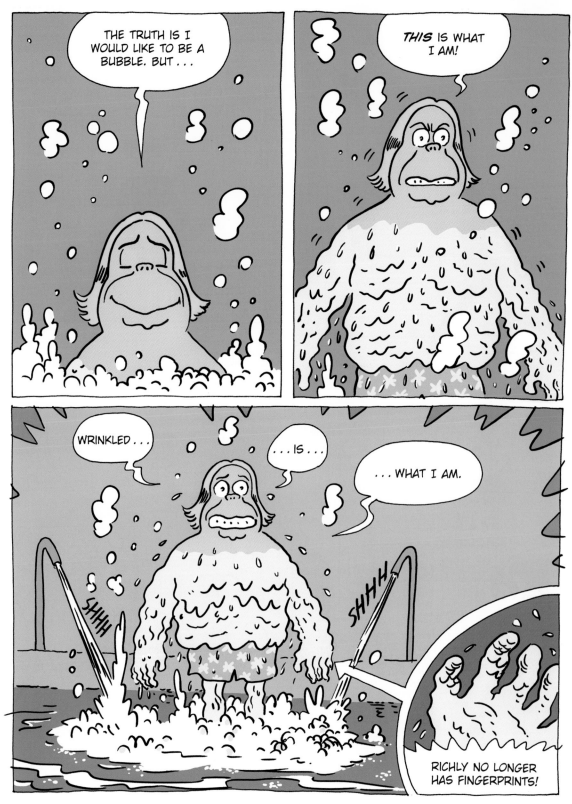

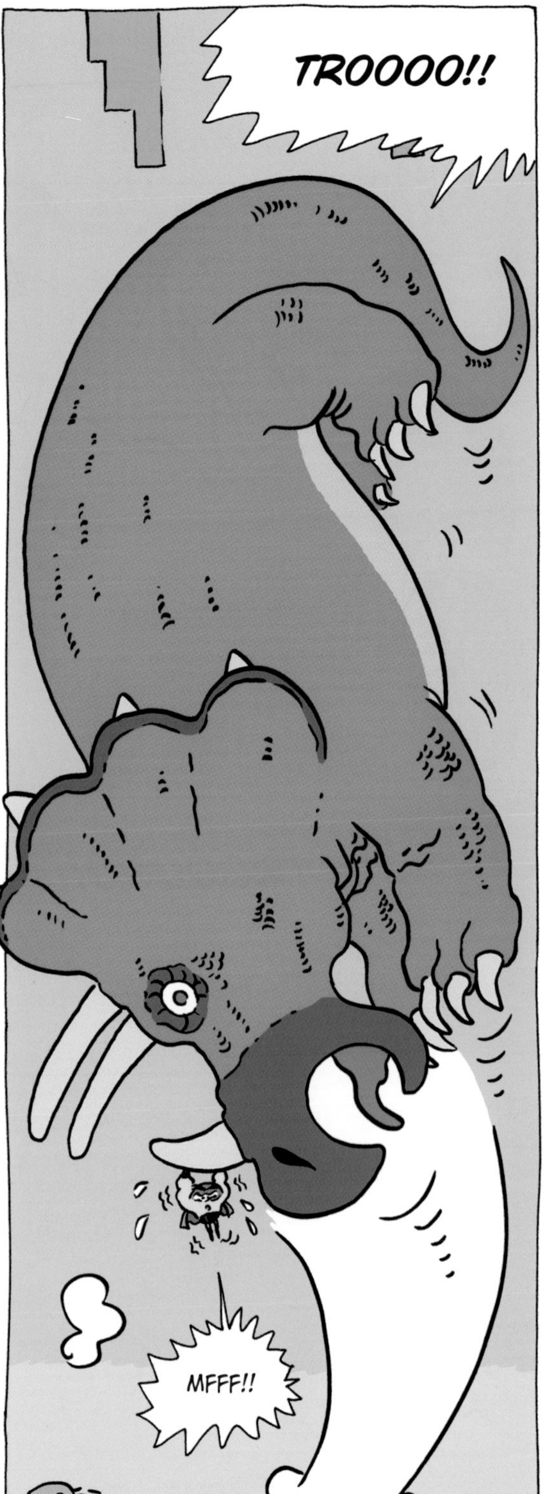
TROOOO!!
MFFF!!

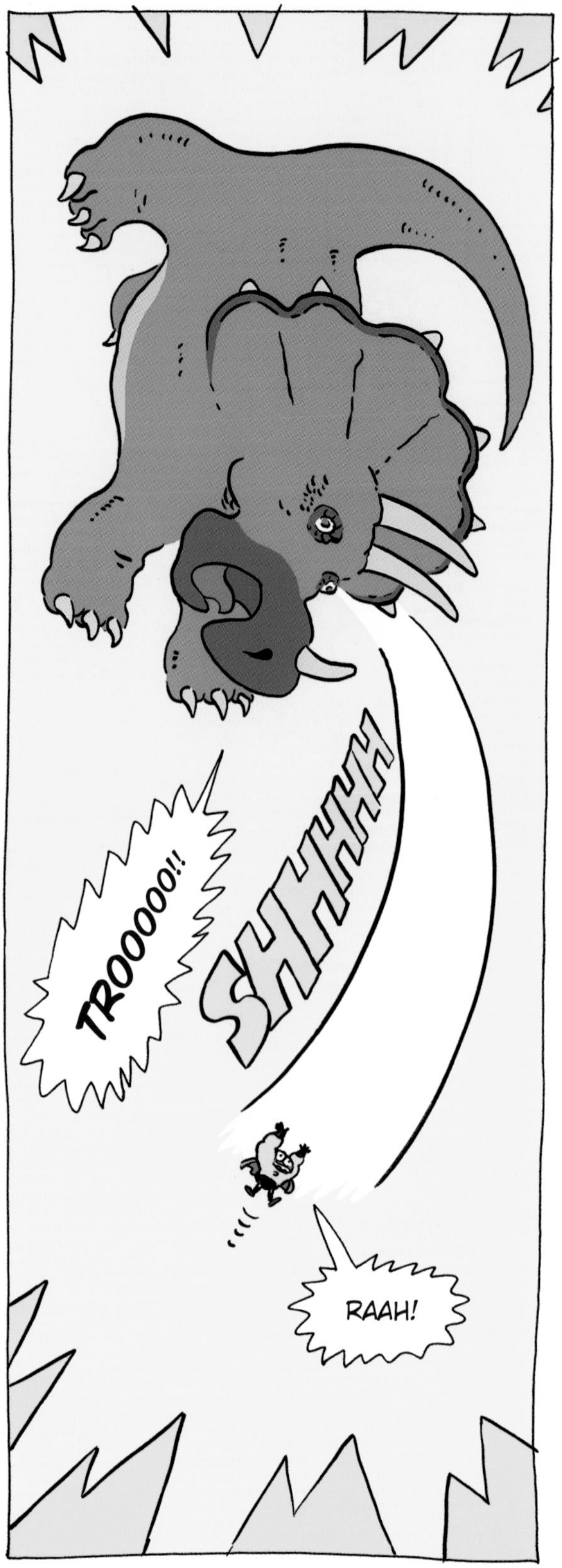
TROOOOO!!
SHHHHH
RAAH!

41

43

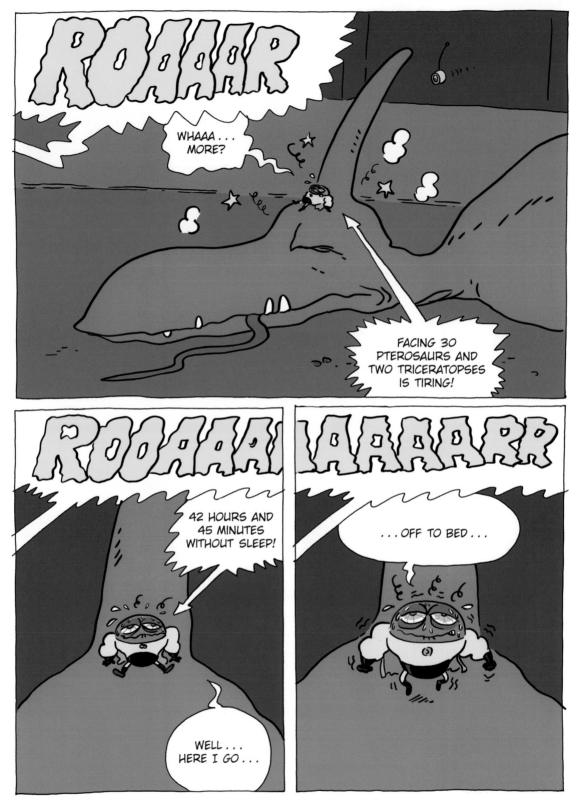

44

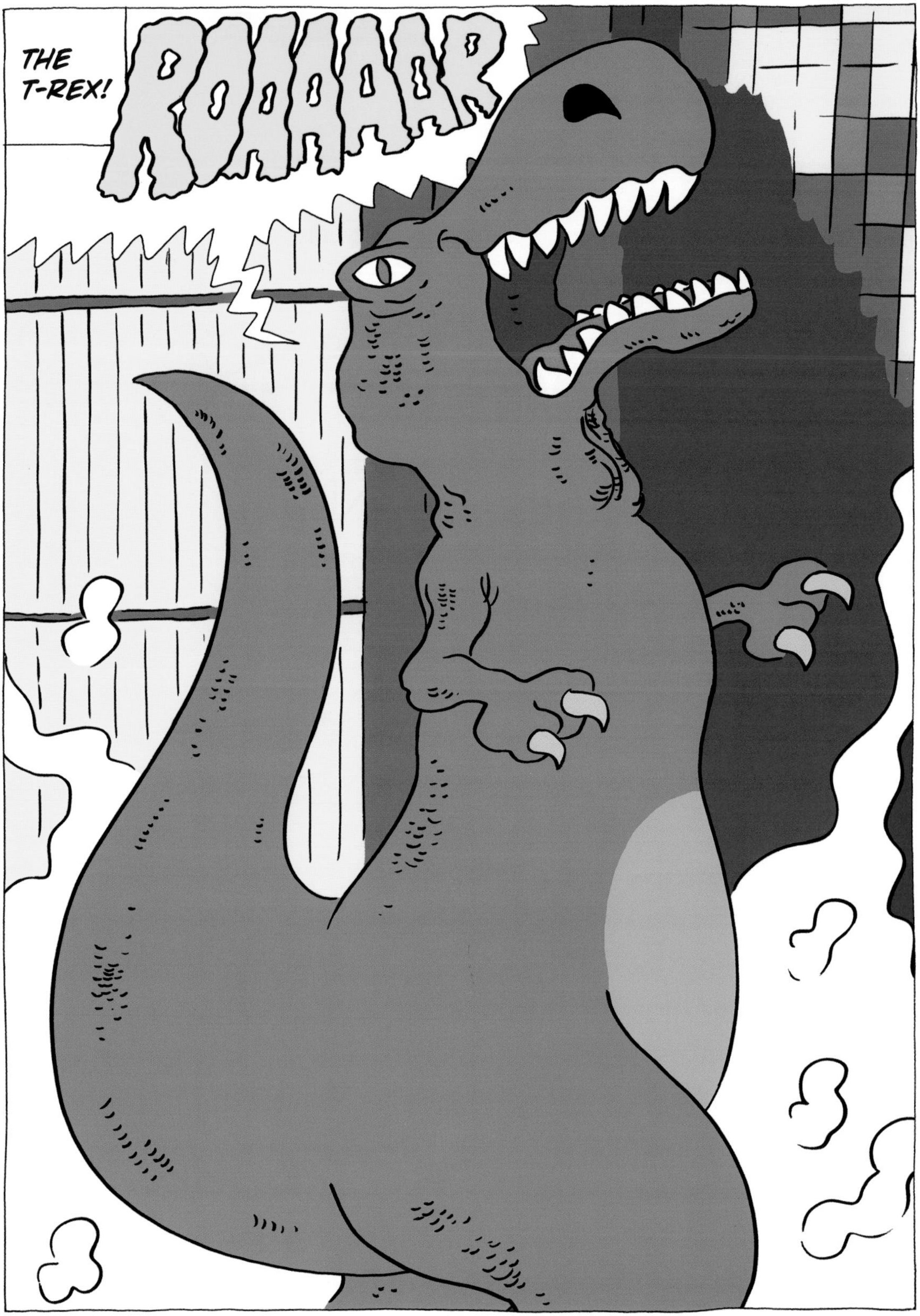
THE T-REX!
ROAAAAR

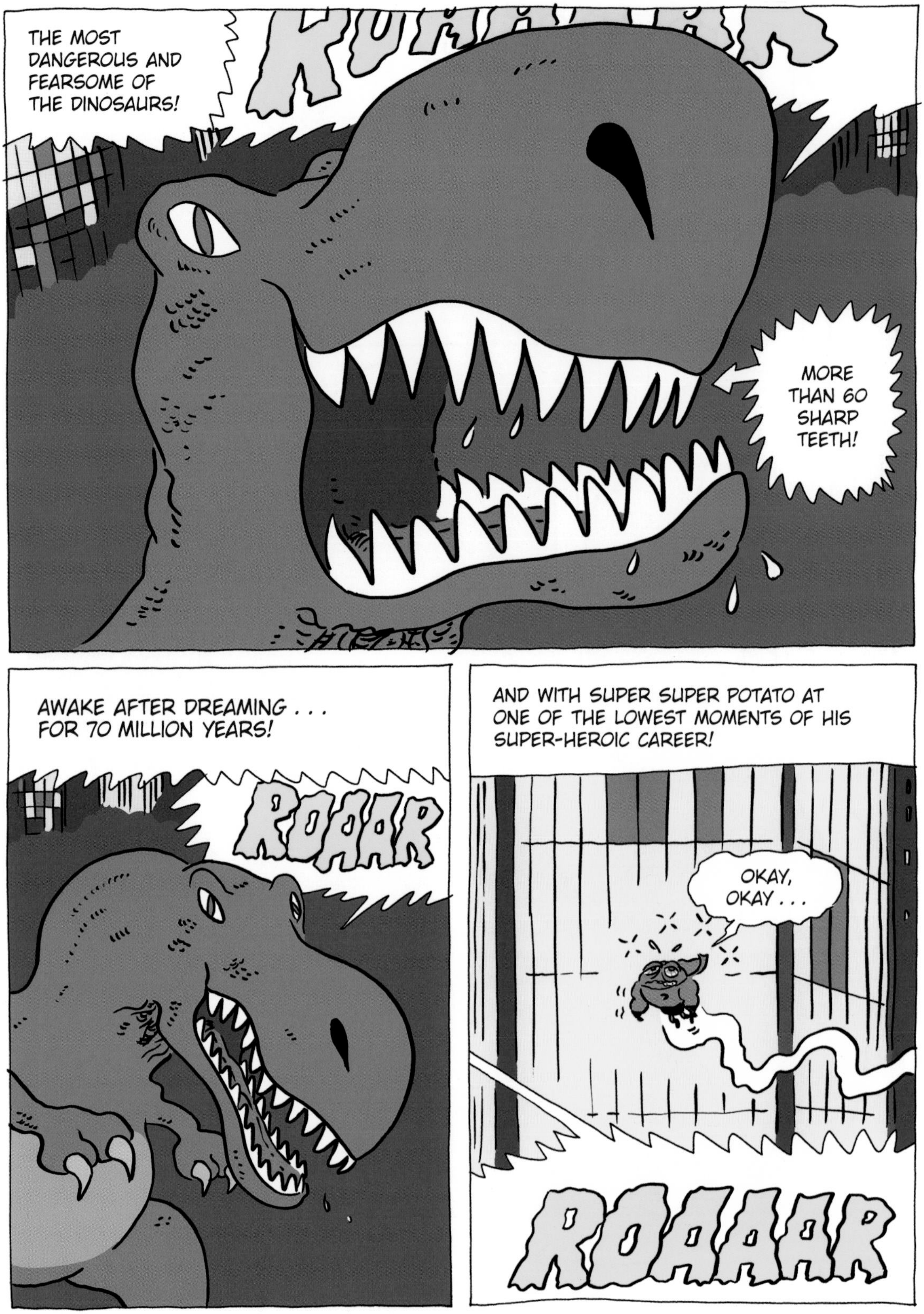
THE MOST DANGEROUS AND FEARSOME OF THE DINOSAURS!
MORE THAN 60 SHARP TEETH!
AWAKE AFTER DREAMING . . . FOR 70 MILLION YEARS!
ROAAR
AND WITH SUPER SUPER POTATO AT ONE OF THE LOWEST MOMENTS OF HIS SUPER-HEROIC CAREER!
OKAY, OKAY . . .
ROAAAR

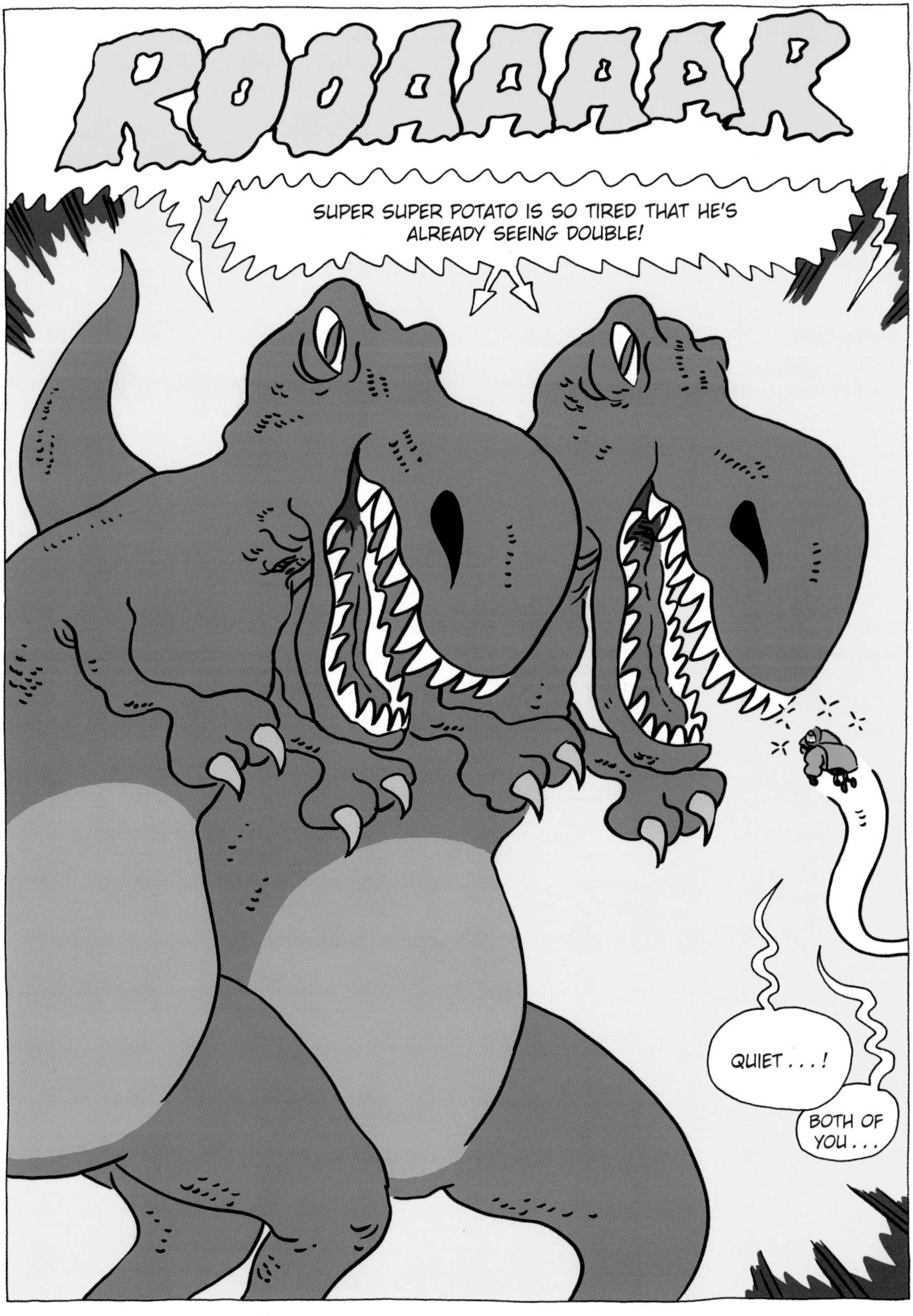
ROOAAAAR
SUPER SUPER POTATO IS SO TIRED THAT HE'S ALREADY SEEING DOUBLE!
QUIET . . . !
BOTH OF YOU . . .

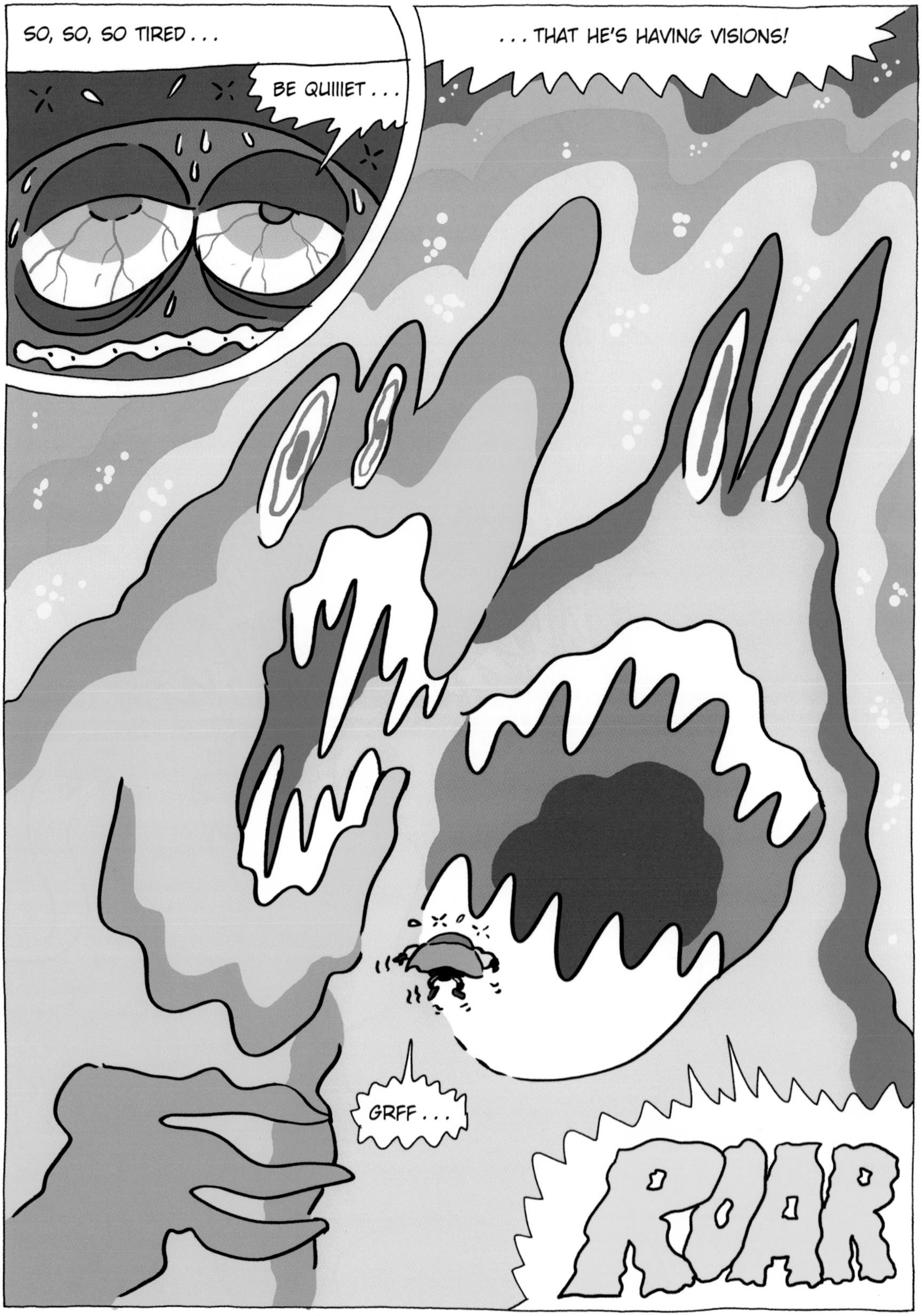
SO, SO, SO TIRED . . .
BE QUIIIET . . .
. . . THAT HE'S HAVING VISIONS!
GRFF . . .
ROAR

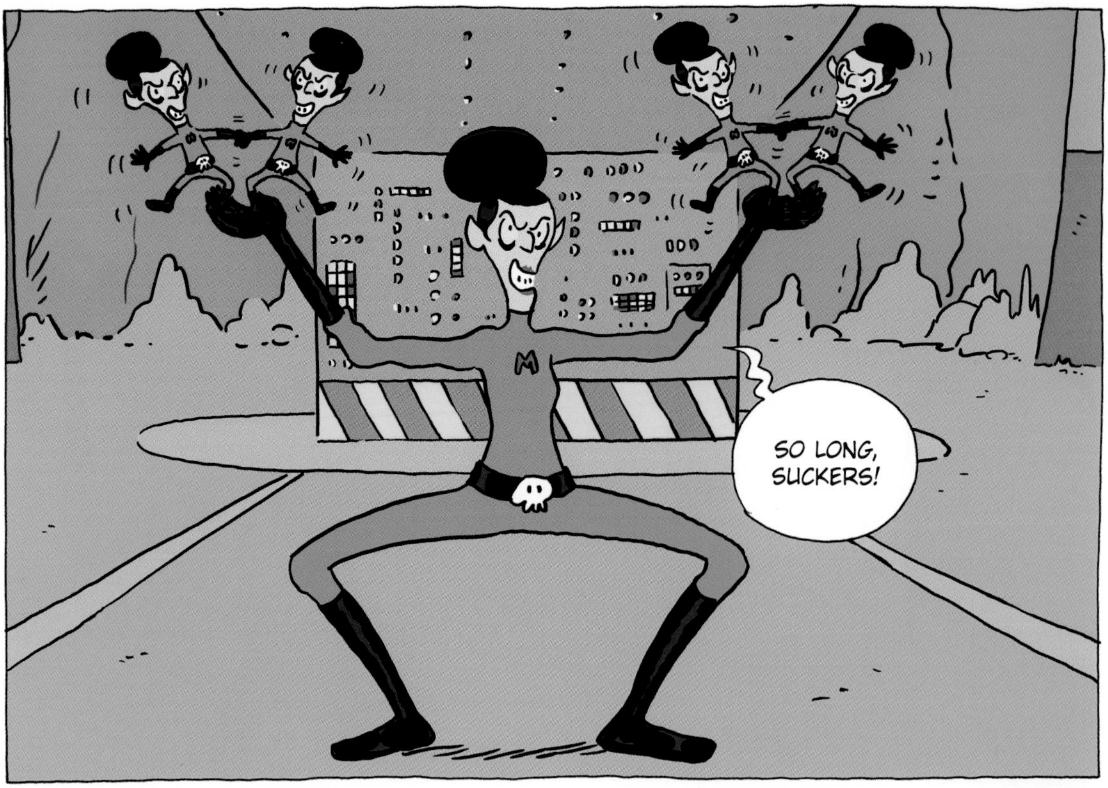
SO LONG, SUCKERS!

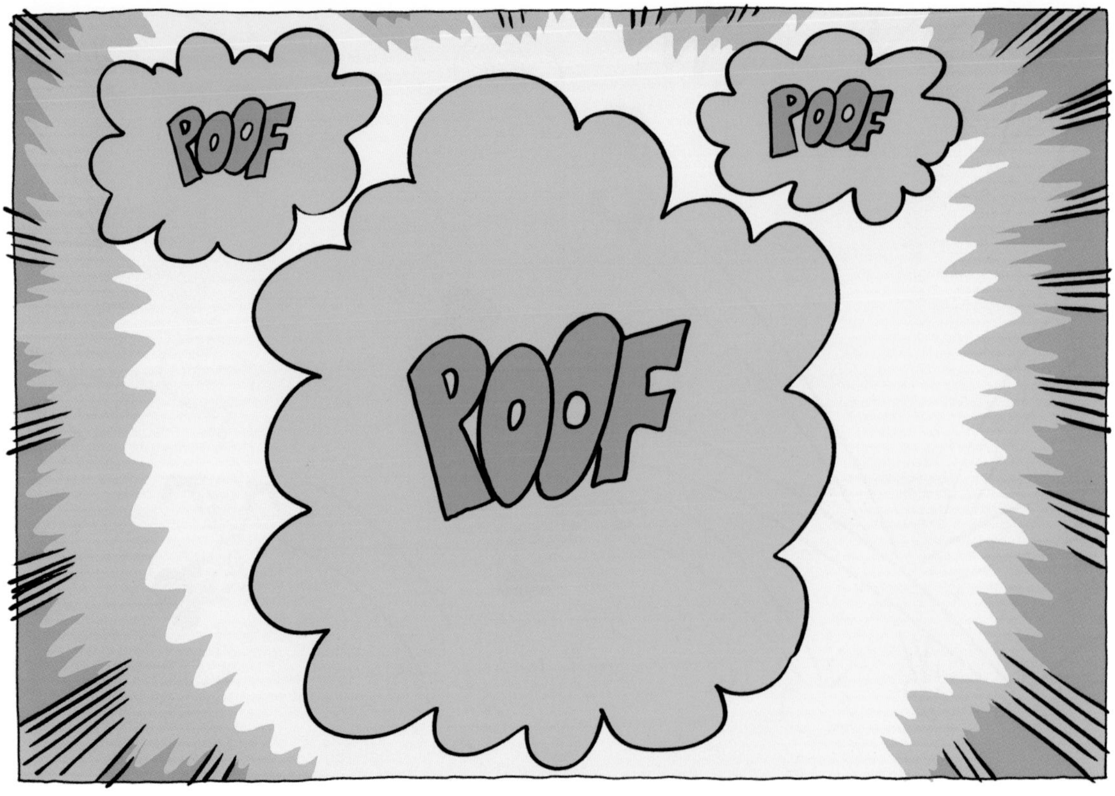
POOF
POOF
POOF

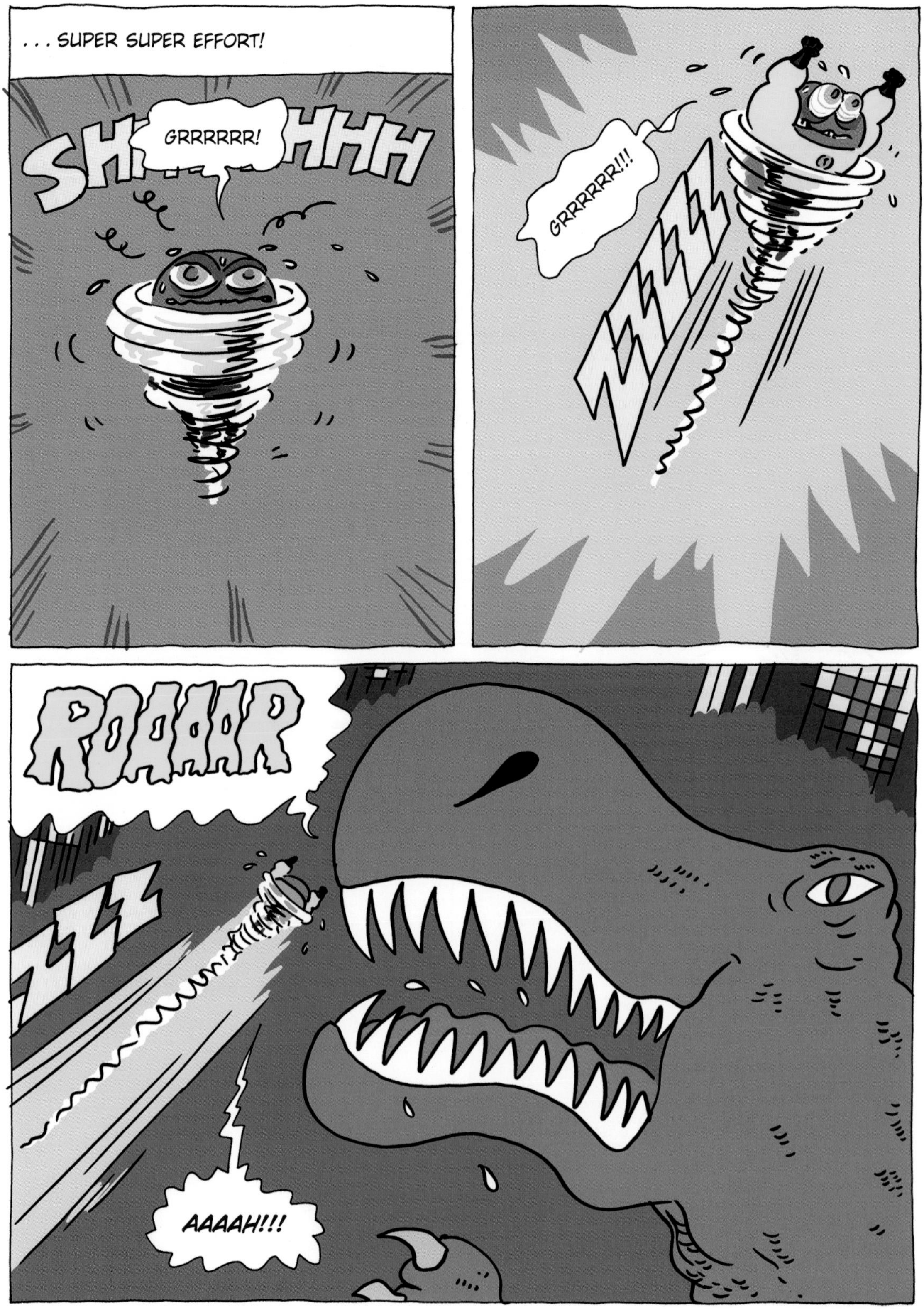
. . . SUPER SUPER EFFORT!
GRRRRRR!
GRRRRRR!!!
ROAAAR
AAAAH!!!

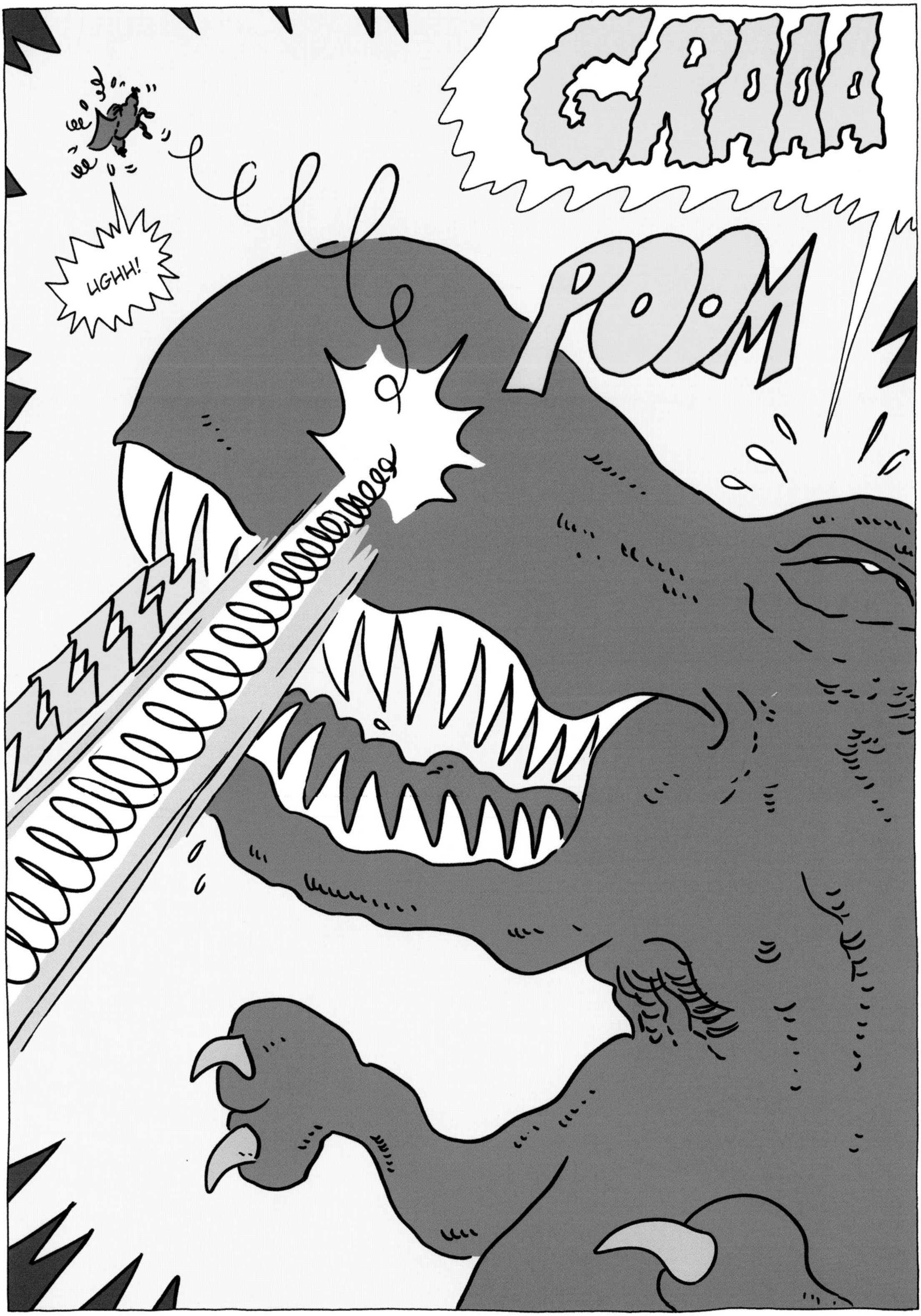
UGHH!
GRAAA
POOM

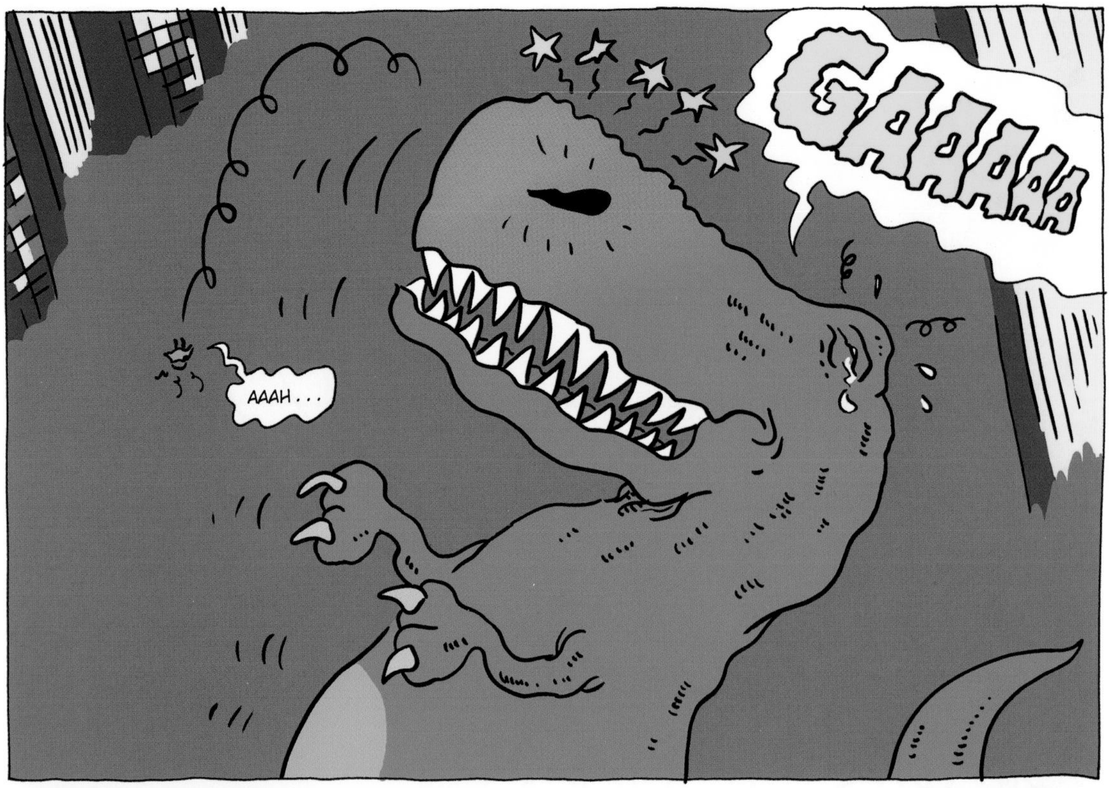
GAAAAA
AAAH...

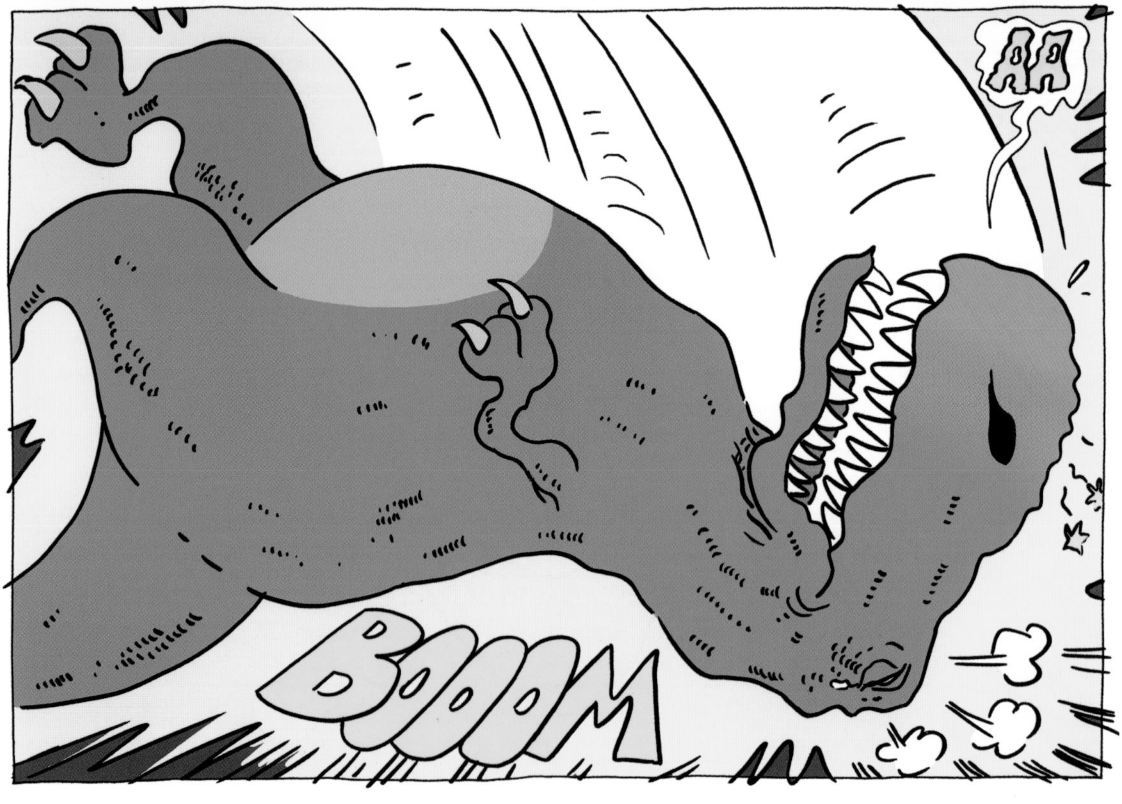
AA
BOOOM

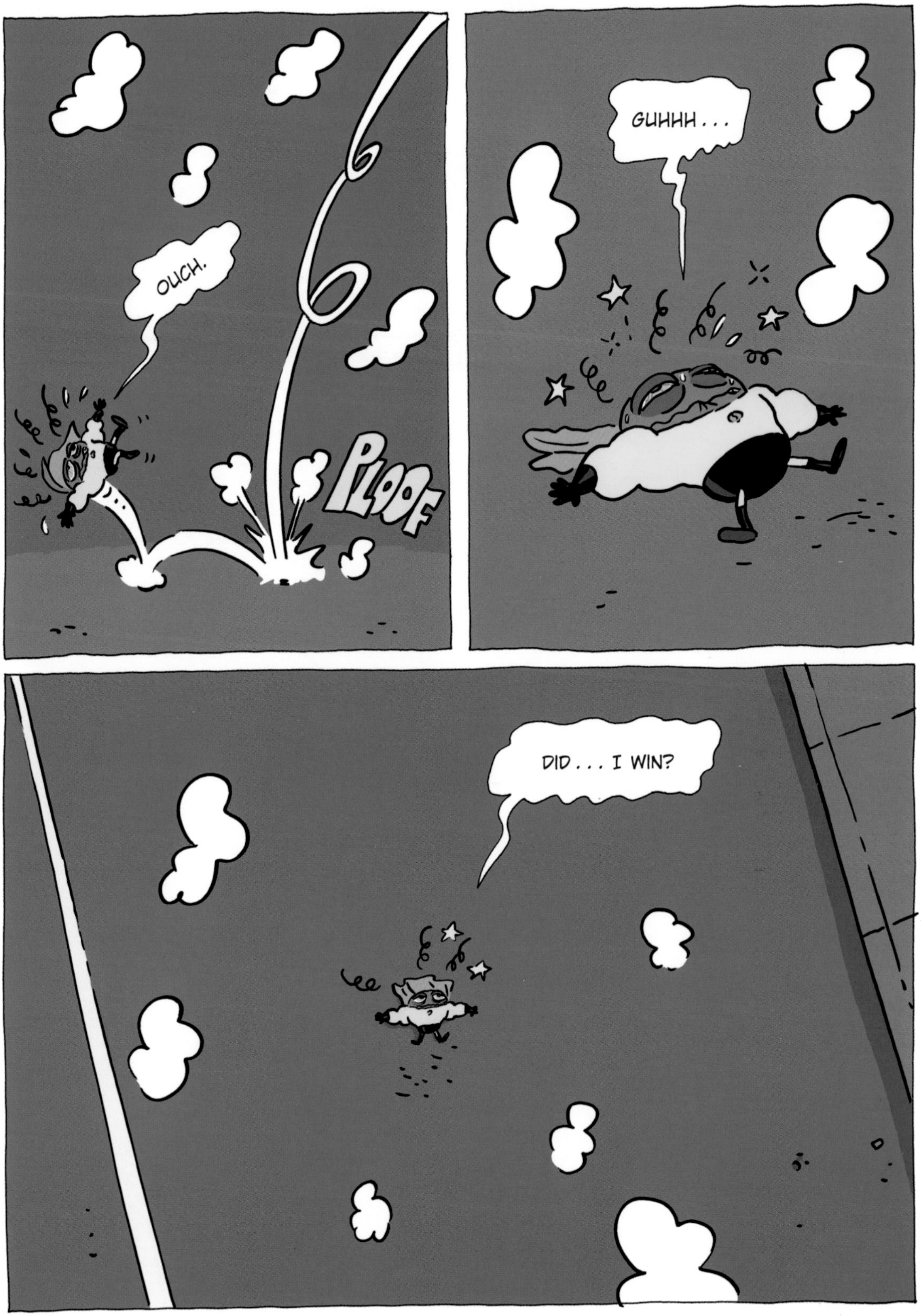
OUCH.
PLOOF
GUHHH . . .
DID . . . I WIN?

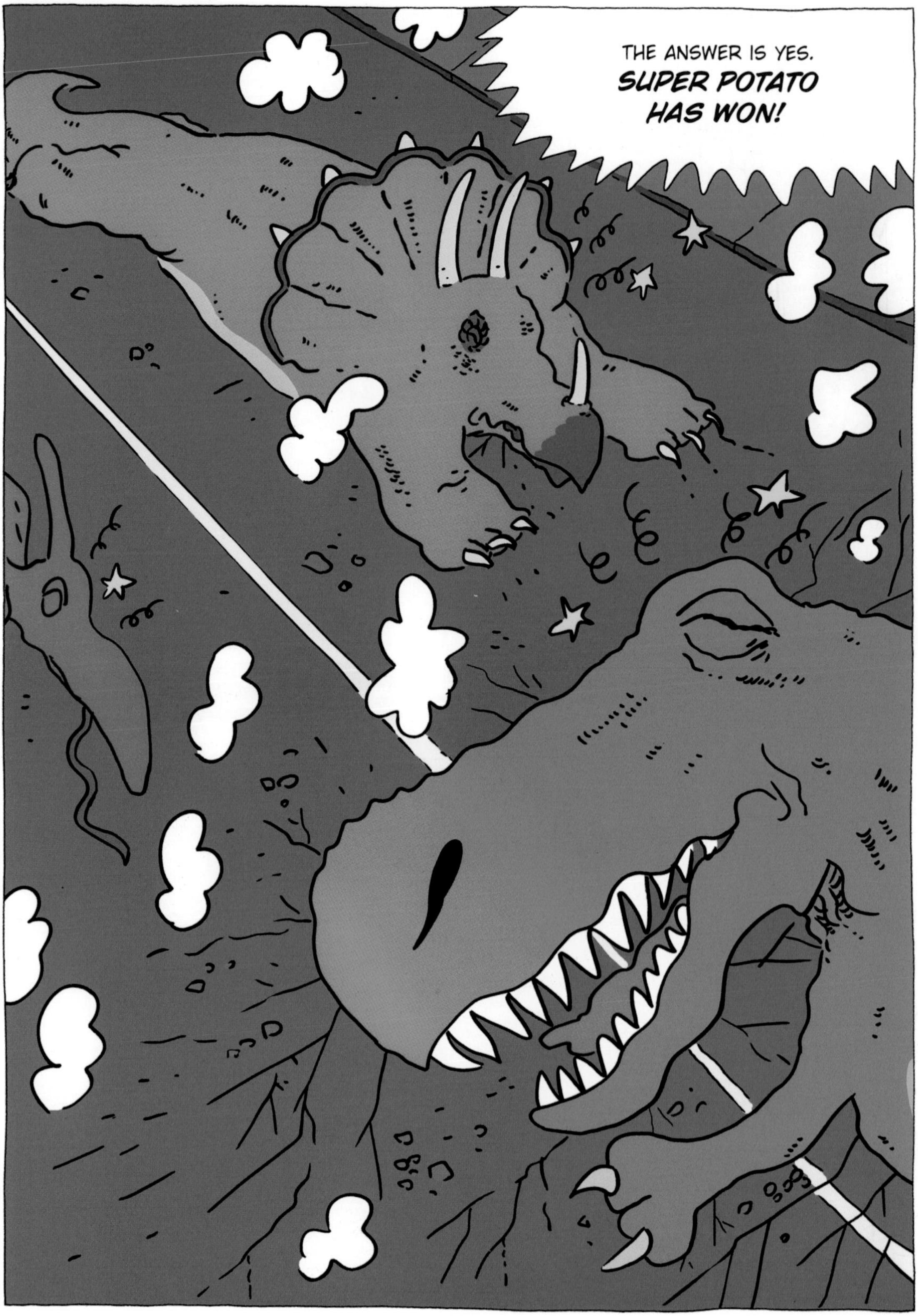
THE ANSWER IS YES.
SUPER POTATO HAS WON!

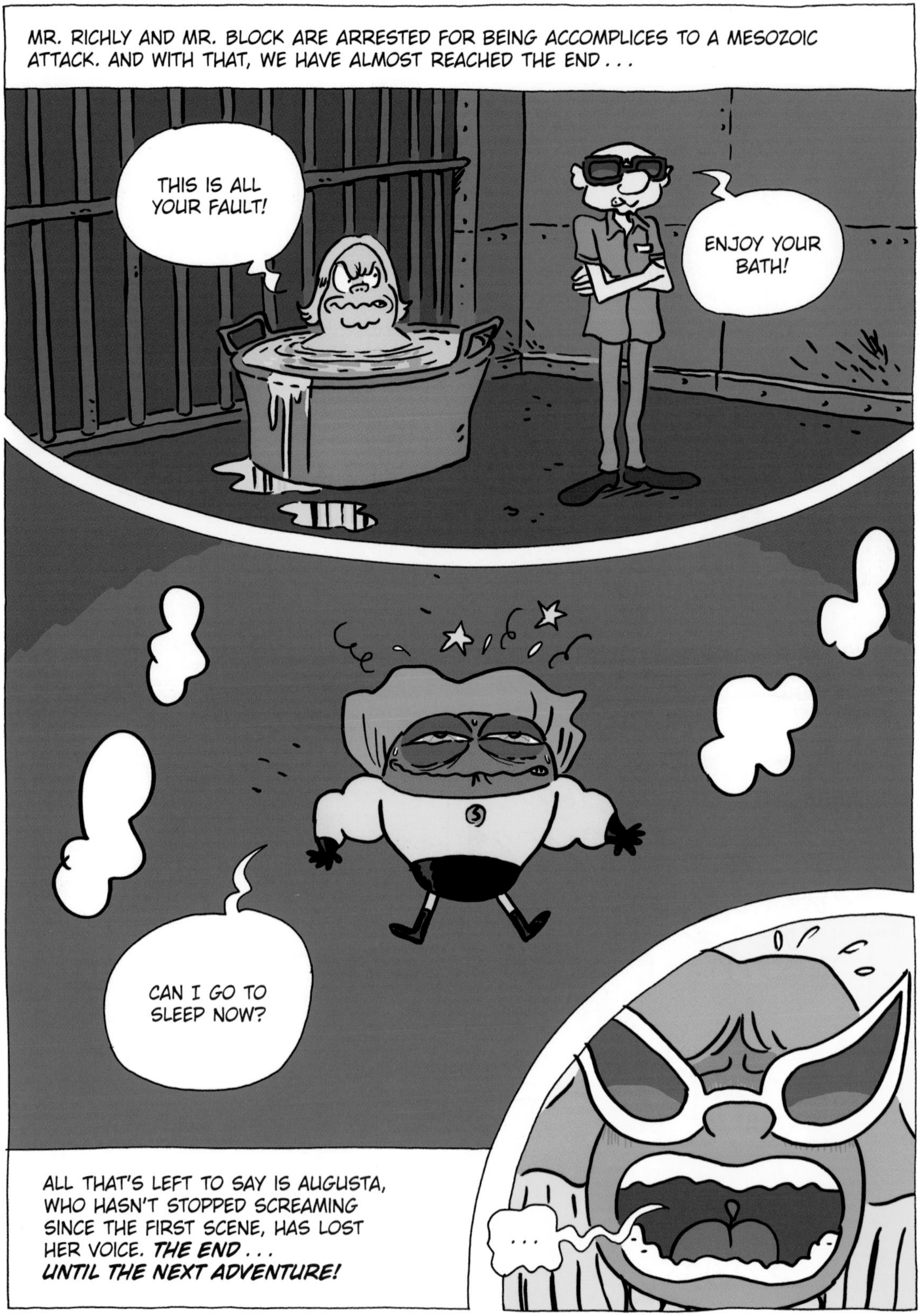
MR. RICHLY AND MR. BLOCK ARE ARRESTED FOR BEING ACCOMPLICES TO A MESOZOIC ATTACK. AND WITH THAT, WE HAVE ALMOST REACHED THE END . . .
THIS IS ALL YOUR FAULT!
ENJOY YOUR BATH!
CAN I GO TO SLEEP NOW?
ALL THAT'S LEFT TO SAY IS AUGUSTA, WHO HASN'T STOPPED SCREAMING SINCE THE FIRST SCENE, HAS LOST HER VOICE. *THE END . . . UNTIL THE NEXT ADVENTURE!*
. . .

For more hilarious tales of Super Potato, check out . . .

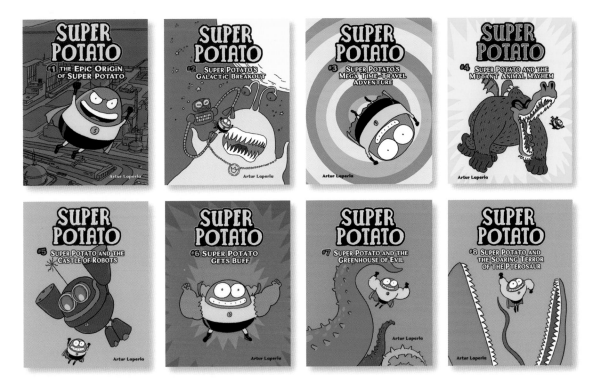

AND TURN THE PAGE FOR A PREVIEW OF OUR HERO'S NEXT ADVENTURE . . .